HUNTER KILLER

CASTALIA HOUSE

MILITARY SCIENCE FICTION
Wardogs #1: Battlesuit Bastards by G. D. Stark
Wardogs #2: Hunter Killer by G. D. Stark
Wardogs #3: Metal Monsters by G. D. Stark
Starship Liberator by David VanDyke and B. V. Larson
Battleship Indomitable by David VanDyke and B. V. Larson
The Eden Plague by David VanDyke
Reaper's Run by David VanDyke
Skull's Shadows by David VanDyke

SCIENCE FICTION
Quantum Mortis: A Man Disrupted by Vox Day
The End of the World as We Knew It by Nick Cole
CTRL-ALT REVOLT! by Nick Cole
Pop Kult Warlord by Nick Cole
Soda Pop Soldier by Nick Cole
Back From the Dead by Rolf Nelson
Mutiny in Space by Rod Walker
Alien Game by Rod Walker
Young Man's War by Rod Walker

FICTION
Turned Earth: A Jack Broccoli Novel by David T. Good
An Equation of Almost Infinite Complexity by J. Mulrooney
The Promethean by Owen Stanley
The Missionaries by Owen Stanley

FANTASY
Summa Elvetica by Vox Day
A Throne of Bones by Vox Day
A Sea of Skulls by Vox Day

NON-FICTION
Corporate Cancer by Vox Day
Jordanetics by Vox Day
The Last Closet by Moira Greyland
4th Generation Warfare Handbook by William S. Lind and Gregory A. Thiele
Appendix N: A Literary History of Dungeons & Dragons by Jeffro Johnson

QUANTUM MORTIS

WARDOGS

HUNTER KILLER

G.D. STARK

CASTALIA HOUSE

Hunter Killer

G.D. Stark

Published by Castalia House
Tampere, Finland
www.castaliahouse.com

Cover: Steve Beaulieu
Editor: Vox Day
Created by Vox Day

ISBN: 978-952-7065-09-9

Contents

Chapter 1

"It's natural, then?" Jones pressed.

The girl on the left cocked an eyebrow at him. *If I know women,* I'd say the look on her finely featured pale-blue face was getting closer to irritation than desire. But those legs! *Come on, Jones—don't scare them off.*

"I mean, I used to know this gal with purple eyes," he continued casually. "The white part, you know. But it was some sort of ink. She put it in with needles."

Both girls winced but Jones pressed on. "Blue skin, though. That's really exotic."

"Jones," I jumped in, "they're Achernaran. Right ladies?"

"Mmmhmm," said the second girl, focusing on us for a moment. She'd been staring off into the distance, her corneas twitching now and again as she looked at whatever her personal augment was feeding her. "You know about Achernar?"

"Oh yeah," I lied. "It's even nicer than here. Great swimming."

"Here" was Kookooma, a tropical island nation on Kantillon. 402 sun days a year with pink sand beaches and bars, casinos and techno clubs as far as the eye could see. We were taking a much-needed break from killing people to soak up a little sun and play a few games—and hopefully to get laid, provided Jones didn't screw it up.

"You didn't worry about screwlice?" the girl asked quizzically.

"What?" I said.

"Offworlders don't usually go in the water."

"Oh right," I said. "I swam in the hotel pool. It was huge."

"So," said Jones to his target. "You're blue all over?"

She rolled her eyes.

"I knew it," Jones said, eying her cleavage. She had small, perfect breasts like robin eggs, safely nestled in a cream bikini top. "You just can't be too sure these days. Lots of fakes wandering around."

"I'm sure," she said. Her friend yawned and went back to twitching her corneas.

"Hi ladies," came a voice from behind us. "These boys bothering you?"

"Actually, we were supposed to meet someone," said the jacked girl, taking cream bikini by the elbow and guiding her away. I watched their swaying hips recede with a wistful sigh.

"Frigging cockblock," Jones said, wheeling on Ward.

Ward laughed. "Like you had a chance. My three-year-old is better at chatting up chicks."

"Your three-year-old is going to be an orphan," Jones said.

Ward shrugged. "At least he'll inherit a few bucks, unlike any kids you may have spawned."

"Low blow," I said. "Just because you won a little on the tables and we got shafted doesn't mean you get to screw up the rest of our day."

I was down a few thousand credits and Jones was down at least that much.

"A little? Try a couple grand," Ward said, studying his fingernails.

"I'll couple grand you," Jones said.

"I think someone needs a margarita," Ward grinned, waving down a passing waitress. "Three margaritas." She nodded and disappeared. The drinks arrived quickly and we drank and shot the breeze for an hour or so, soaking in the ambience, eating artery-clogging appetizers and eying the girls.

An indeterminate number of drinks later, we walked out out along the seawall and found a picnic table by the ocean where we could watch the sunset. The breeze had picked up, salty and fresh.

"They say it flashes green when it hits the ocean," Ward said.

"It doesn't hit the ocean," Jones said, slurring a little. "It goes around the planet."

"No it doesn't, retard," Ward said.

"You know what I mean," Jones said.

"It's going in," Ward said, as the gold disk sank slowly into the ocean. We watched until it was a sliver, then it was gone. I looked but I didn't see a flash.

"Did you see a flash?" I asked Ward.

He shook his head. "Maybe it's not all the time."

"I want a girl that's blue all over," Jones said, putting his head down on the table. "Or two."

"Actually," I said, spotting our previous targets, "they're over there."

They were walking up to the railing accompanied by a thin guy in tight jeans and hair that stuck straight up. He had them laughing at some joke, the little weasel.

"Some faggot has taken my place," Jones said.

"I'm going in," I announced, and tapped Jones on the shoulder. "You stay here." He muttered something, his eyes shut.

The girls had seen me. Cream bikini gave me a little wave. Hey, I did still have it. I stood up—only a bit unsteady—and started towards them, enjoying the suddenly suspicious look on the skinny guy's face. He had no idea what was coming.

"Tommy," came a voice as a hand was clasped on my shoulder. *Dammit—who now?* Then I started. It was Captain Marks. "Captain!" I said. "Hey, I…"

He followed my eyes to the girls and shook his head. *Dammit!*

"I got something better," he said, directing me back to our table. "Jones, wake up," he said, rapping his knuckles on the sleeping man's head. Jones woke with a start and pulled back his fist to hit his assailant, then quickly dropped it when he saw who it was.

"What's up, Captain?" he asked.

"Money," he told us. "You guys looking for any?"

Two hours and a couple of AntiAlc tablets later, I sat in an air-conditioned conference room with Jones, Ward and Zelag. Jack Zelag was a new operator who had missed the fun on Ulixis due to the tech restraints. I looked at his silver right arm. Supposedly they wired the artificial limbs right into your head and the sensors were better than real skin, but still—I imagined stroking creme bikini's silky back with that metallic hand. No way would that feel right! I'd probably just get a new flesh-and-blood arm before I went for a robotic one, but I knew that some guys loved their augments. The robo-arm aside, Zelag was supposed to be a bit of a loose cannon. I'd seen him around before, but I didn't know him. Ward said Zelag collected old handguns, though, so I figured he'd at least be a good shot.

Jones sipped at a mug of hard coffee as Ward bit his nails.

"It's good money," I said, breaking the silence.

"Yeah, but is it too good?" Ward said. After Ulixis, we were all feeling suspicious of anything that looked too easy to be true. Then Captain Marks walked in.

"Looks like the answer is here," Zelag said as we stood in unison.

"At ease, gentlemen," the captain said. "Sit down and I'll fill you in. Three of you were chosen for your excellent performance on Ulixis, and Zelag, I guess they picked you because someone in accounting has a fetish for missing limbs."

We laughed, then Marks put up a hand to silence us.

"Now," the Captain continued, "here's the mission. The Datacon-Verlaag GmbH corporation had a bit of an issue at their Feymanus branch yesterday, so the local CEO of operations needs some body-guards until things blow over."

"A bit of an issue, sir?" Ward asked.

"See for yourself," Marks said, engaging the viewscreen behind him with a motion of his hand. On it appeared a high-resolution security camera image of a stretch of cafes and markets. A small booth with trays of what looked like olives was front and center, an older man sitting behind it in an antigrav chair. Up walked a guy in a suit, sipping a drink through a straw.

"That's the victim," Marks said. "Albert Fast."

The man looked to the side as a woman came up to the booth beside him. He was maybe in his 40s, clean-shaven with good hair. His suit looked tailored. The old man offered both him and the woman a sample of the olives. He accepted, the woman declined. Then the woman reached in her purse as if she were going to pay for something, but instead produced a small cylinder and stabbed it into the victim's side.

"Stunpen," Zelag muttered.

The man moved back as if confused by the woman's actions, then put his arms up as she stabbed him at him again and again, finally landing a clean injection. The guy went down, pulling at the edge of the tablecloth and falling in a mess of upended olive trays. Then the woman made some strange hand movements towards the heavens. It looked like she was trying to make shadow puppets. A second later, she ran out of frame.

The old guy jumped up and looked over the counter, yelling for help. The guy in the suit was motionless. The screen went blank and Marks spoke.

"There's our incident," he said. "She stabbed him with a stunpen loaded with cyanide, then made her little hand movement and ran off."

"They catch her?" Ward asked.

"Yes," said the captain. "She's a Chrysalan. Some call them the Sky People."

"What the hell?" Jones said.

"It's a cult," Zelag said. "They believe people are like caterpillars, waiting to enter their cocoons, after which they come out as butter-flies full of heavenly energy. It's supposed to be based on an ancient illustrated manuscript published on Old Earth."

"You've got the gist of it," said Captain Marks, surprised.

"So why did she kill the guy?" I asked.

"A minor miscalculation on his part," Marks said. "He was the marketing director who oversaw their latest ad campaign. It featured Mt. Xirtis, contained various testimonials to the company's high level of data security, then the tagline 'come to the mountain.'"

We listened, confused. Marks saw our looks and tried to explain. "It's a metaphor, you see."

"So these caterpillar people hate metaphors?" Ward said, puzzled.

"Or they hate skiing?" Jones volunteered.

"Skiing is actually prohibited on Mt. Xirtis," Marks said. "Along with every other sporting activity. Because it's considered to be a 'holy mountain.'" He made quotation marks with his fingers when he said it.

"To the Chrysalans," I mused.

"Bingo," Marks said. "The marketing department basically claimed their data protection company was on par with the sacred mountain of the gods. The temple of the sky is at the base of the mountain and there is a massive pilgrimage that travels up the mountain once a year."

"Oh yeah," Zelag said. "I watched a documentary. The really serious ones go without oxygen all the way to the top."

"Sure you're not one of them, Zelag?" Ward said.

Zelag shook his head. "I hate bugs. And mountain climbing."

"So that woman killed the head of marketing because of some stupid advertising?" Jones said.

"That's not the first time," Zelag said. "A few years back they threw acid in the face of a pop singer for recording a song called 'Like a Butterfly.'"

"Geez," Jones said. "That's pretty hard core."

"I wouldn't say that," Ward said. "That assassin did a lousy job of it. She didn't even get a good stab on him the first time. He could have just pushed her away if he'd known it was coming."

"Amateur hour," Marks agreed. "Nevertheless, DVG is concerned about the safety of their local CEO on Feymanus, a gentleman by the name of Brixton Heiermach. They have contracted with WDI to keep him safe. As you know, there are few things that put the righteous fear of God into evil-minded folks like a team of Wardogs bodyguards."

"How long does he need hand-holding?" I asked. It looked like a pretty damn easy job to me.

"Good question," Marks replied. "It could take a while, but DVG is actively working on damage control already. Heiermach plans to offer a sincere corporate apology to the Chrysalans, as well as pledge funds to refurbish the ancient temple at the base of the mountain. Still—the longer it takes, the more money you make. Glorified babysitting."

"Wait a minute," Jones said. "The CEO is going to apologize to these caterpillar cultists after they murdered his marketing director?"

Marks shrugged. "Apparently an angry mob has also scrawled pictures of butterflies on multiple DVG office buildings and spent three days beating drums, chanting and pissing sacred streams of their holy urine on the steps to claim the infidel's earthly property for the sky."

"Judeo-Christ," I muttered.

"Can we nuke them?" Jones asked.

I thought Marks' mouth almost twitched towards a grin at the suggestion, but I might have been wrong. He was good at being serious. "No," Marks said. "We're not launching a crusade against these people, we're just protecting a businessman. Unlike you bastards, DVG has to deal with the public on a regular basis. It's an old and well-respected religion on the planet, and they have some highly connected members on Feymanus. And their extremists have been implicated in just enough acts of terror that no one wants to set them off unnecessarily."

"And so we play bodyguard to Mr. Heiermach," Jones said. "No big deal. Crazy chicks with stunpens don't keep me awake at night."

Marks nodded. "Tommy, you'll be in charge this time out. Think you can handle it?"

"Yessir," I said. "Though I'm not as qualified as Sergeant Hanley."

"He's on leave. And this is cake—the experience will be good for you. You did well on Ulixis and I think you have a bright future."

"Who's my boss on Feymanus?" I asked.

"Captain Elrich Williams. System VP. He's a busy man so don't waste his time if you don't have to. We'll be able to supply you in New Patras from a branch office. Check in when you get there and we'll make sure you have everything you need."

He stood and opened the door. "Now go sign your docs in HR. You leave within the hour."

Chapter 2

"Perhaps we should have looked farther afield," Heiermach said, waving his hand at the view behind him, then taking a sip from his coffee. I sat with Jones, Zelag, Ward and the local Wardogs salesman who had set up this arrangement. Jim Pinkers. Bald guy, short, smiling and gentlemanly. One of the small army of guys that raked in cash for us. We'd met him at the spaceport and then stopped by the local WDI office and gotten briefed and hooked up with some nice next-gen battlesuits, still smelling like the factory. After lunch, we suited up and he and a driver brought us to the main DVG office. Now we sat in a sweeping conference room at a kidney-shaped table. Our job was to look intimidating and impressive, and we rocked the look, if I say so myself.

Outside I could hear the sound of chanting. The local police had cordoned off the front of the building but a knot of stubborn Chrysalans were out there, wailing and gnashing their teeth. When we'd come up the front steps in our armor, the small crowd had melted away like butter. Our slate gray and pearly white armor was unmistakable even if you missed the Wardogs logo on the chest. I gotta say, it's a kick getting to wear the uniform in an urban area. Especially amidst a bunch of hippie rabble like the losers surrounding DVG HQ. I noticed a lot of the protesters had shaved heads and tattoos on their faces. Great. Made them easier to spot.

"We could have focused on the stars, or a generic cloud logo," Heiermach continued. "Some of the boys put together a very nice campaign based on a water molecule. 'It just fits,' was the tagline. Problem was, the molecule looks like the logo of a powerful entertainment conglomerate. And really, trying to link our brand with chemistry lacked a certain… chemistry, I guess you could say. So the mountain it was. We've been headquartered here for a century. That mountain over there belongs to us as much as anyone else. 'Come to the mountain' is really solid copy. And you're literally coming to the mountain—or near the mountain—when you work with DVG. This whole thing has been more than unfortunate."

"Extremism is so ugly," Pinkers said.

"Worse, it's bad for business," said Heiermach. He sighed. "Also, Fast was a friend of mine. I was at his daughter's wedding three months ago."

"Our condolences," Pinkers said. "Truly a tragedy. We're glad you've brought us on board. Our men will ensure that you do not share his lamentable fate."

"I'm sure," Heiermach said, looking at each of us in turn. "An imposing quartet indeed. I'll wager your boys could kill me thirty different ways in less than a jiffy."

We didn't say anything. It was true.

"Oh, don't say that. You're our client, Mr. Heiermach," Pinkers quickly protested. "Their job is to kill the bad guys, should it prove necessary."

"Of course," said Heiermach. "But I really don't want any trouble. Acquiring a reliable bodyguard is one load off my mind but I'm in a delicate PR situation right now. I'm hoping the next couple of weeks will ensure there's no more trouble with the Chrysalans. You know about the apology, right?"

We nodded our assent.

"You'll be there, I assume," Heiermach continued. "I've never had a bodyguard before, let along four."

"That's correct," our salesman said. "They'll be with you around the clock until DVG is certain you are no longer in danger."

"Even in my townhome?" Heiermach said. "I mean, can I take a shower by myself?"

The salesman smiled. "You set the boundaries, sir. You're the client."

"Of course," said Heiermach. "I work hard and I don't like distractions, but I appreciate what you're trying to do. I'm just glad my family isn't here yet."

"You have family?" Ward asked.

"Yes," said the CEO. "Two daughters and my wife. On Rhysalan. I only took this job six months ago—the children are finishing the school year, then they'll all join me. I picked out a good house. It's flat here, though, except for the mountain. Not like where I grew up. Damn that mountain! Such a stupid and unnecessary blunder! Anyhow—that's enough about me. I've got several meetings today. Will your boys just be sitting around my office or what?"

Our salesman smiled. "No, Mr. Heiermach. They'll be placed strategically. When you go outside, they will accompany you. We'll also be monitoring all visitors, as I'm sure your security is doing already. To get to you, a cultist will have to come through the Wardogs first. And no one is going to do that."

At this, Jones mimed cracking his knuckles. Heiermach smiled slightly.

"Excellent," he said. "Even if the board of trustees is simply doing this to keep our stock from plunging in the case of my assassination, I'd rather not end up dead under a pile of olives like Bertie."

He looked out the window at the mountain and shook his head. "They really should have taken it as a tribute. We had no idea. Anyhow, you men do what you need to do. I'm going into my office." He stood, drank the final sip of his coffee, then tossed the cup in the recycler. "This afternoon a high druid of the Sky People will be visiting. We'll meet right here, and I assume you'll be present?"

"Of course, sir," I replied.

We'd arrived on Feymanus in the early hours of the morning. The trip from Kantillon was a single jump and we spent less than 24 hours in a Wardogs Talos Class light cruiser. The *Komainu* was a sweet ship. A recent model, red, gold and black with teeth painted on the bow. About fifty guys could fit but we were the only passengers other than the crew. The Talos Class came out around the point I quit building plastic models and got interested in various female models so I never actually owned a model of this puppy. I wouldn't mind having the cash for a real cruiser like this, though. I could do the inside with velvet, stick in a pair of bass cannons, maybe a brass pole and some black lights. And a bar. All glass and chrome. I'd leave the paint job on the hull alone, though. People gave Wardogs ships a wide berth.

On the ship I'd jacked in and spent some time researching Feymanus. New Patras was located in the Democratic Technostate of Alexandria. The climate was arid but mild. They grew olives, pomegranates, and dates outside the city, though the farms weren't podunk operations like we saw in Corwistal. These were state-of-the-art industrial agriculture operations. Robotic harvesters, drone fertilization, spider bots crawling beneath the canopy and eliminating weeds with tiny plasma torches—high-tech all the way. The low rainfall made Feymanus a perfect location for some of the ancient crops of Old Earth.

The city itself was climate controlled. Invisible dust shields kept the air clean. It was also humidified by automated systems so your skin didn't crack. The local architecture was mostly tall white towers decorated with cool blue glass windows. I don't know if there was a city code that governed the style of buildings or what, but it was a nice look. The streets were wide with lots of space for pedestrians. Small shops with real people in them were scattered here and there, just like the one where Mr. Fast bit the big one. If they were wealthy enough that human vendors could sit around and shoot the breeze while giving out free samples, they must have been well off. It made more sense to set up vending machines or let droids do the selling, but it looked like this made for more community and was a deliberate local choice. Like going back in time but with all the conveniences of the current era. A deliberate anachronism. The government was wealthy and known for its open market system and ease of incorporation. New Patras was home to multiple international businesses—particularly tech corporations—and also featured a fanciful tri-level golf course designed by the post-anarchomodernist architect Simeon Bastrop. Yep. That's the famous lunatic that later went off his rocker and devoted the rest of his life to designing a space station for whales and other marine life. The golf course apparently worked well, though. According to the computer and tourist sites, the city was a great place. From what we'd seen on the ground so far—other than the whacko cultists—it was pleasant in person as well. The DVG office building was a heckuva joint. Even the chairs looked comfortable, though it would have been a bad idea to try to sit in one while wearing a battlesuit.

The high druid was supposed to arrive at any moment. Pink had long ago left us to our own devices. Ward and I had flipped up our visors and were drinking coffee in a small open office that faced Heiermach's executive office. Jones was downstairs at the entrance and Zelag stood in the secretary's office which joined with Heiermach's.

Office people walked quickly past us without engaging. On jobs like this, we let our armor do the intimidating, keeping our visors down when we were around people.

At my side I carried a Blitz Reaper 3Xi. Despite the intimidating name, the Blitz was a small and subtle handgun. The big advantage was its capacity for wide dispersion, plus a precision targeting filter. I could take down a dining room of people with it without breaking the wine glasses. Some people hated it because you had to remember whether you were on tight or wide, but I was so used to the thumb switch I knew by feel whether the beam would hit one guy or five.

At the moment, I had it on non-lethal. Getting hit would still kill you if I shot you right in the brain, so non-lethal is a stretch—but from across the room, you'd probably just end up flat on your back with second-degree burns and no recollection of your name. Probably.

As much as I prefer to rely upon a solid burst of searing plasma from a Popov-Norinco 60, there's a time and a place to be more subtle. Like when you're in a shiny office building boasting an interior that costs more than the average asteroid mining colony.

Heiermach walked out of his door followed by Zelag. We flipped down our visors and ditched the coffee.

Ward stretched his arms and spoke over my com. "Okay, time to meet the crazies."

We walked down the hall behind Heiermach and entered the conference room and stood along the wall behind him. Jones showed up a moment later, as did a dozen high-ranking DVG employees. Probably marketing and sales guys. A blonde in a knee-length skirt looked at us wide-eyed and whispered something to another girl, who shook her head and shushed her.

A few minutes later, a trio of Chrysalans entered the room. In the middle was the high druid, flanked by two serious-looking monks with shaven heads and blue tattoos on their faces. The high druid was an old guy with leathery skin and a shaggy beard that flowed down through three tight metal bands over his chest. He was painfully thin, with sharp eyes that darted about and alertly took in the surroundings. His robe glittered in a shifting array of colors that dazzled the eyes. His face was also tattooed, the ink faded and blurred by time.

Heiermach bowed respectfully and the druid put his hands in the air and muttered some words, before motioning for everyone to sit. We remained standing, but the old guy ignored us. We were just part of the furniture as far as he was concerned.

"Thank you for coming, Chief Druid Gortanian," Heiermach said politely as we sat. "We have been greatly upset by the pain we have inadvertently caused the members of your faith, and we are very sorry for our actions."

The druid nodded curtly. "Blasphemy against the sacred mountain is a serious affair, and one that cannot be taken lightly."

"Yes," said Heiermach. "So we have gathered."

Heiermach's voice betrayed none of the disdain we knew he harbored for the cultists. He was a true corporate professional, doing his best in a bad situation. A man and a woman came in with a rolling table of refreshments and placed them in the middle of the table, along with a pitcher of water and a carafe of coffee.

"No," said the druid, waving his hands. "Please, tempt me not!"

"Pardon me?" said Heiermach.

"The calendar… this is a time for denial of the flesh—not indulgence!"

"Hee-oo-ARR!" both his companions barked in tandem.

I put my hand on my Reaper but no one made any threatening moves. The two servers quickly removed the refreshments from the table at a nod from Heiermach.

"I have subsisted solely on sunlight for these three days since you contacted me," said the druid. "I cannot permit my mind to be clouded."

Great. Crazy and faint with hunger and thirst was always a combination that spelled out rational behavior. Well, at least we knew the negotiations wouldn't last too long.

"I see," said Heiermach as the servers closed the doors. "I hope that we can resolve this situation as soon as possible so you may return to more substantial fare."

The druid nodded slightly.

"As I hope you now understand," said Heiermach, "we did not intend to cause any offense by using the holy mountain in our advertisements. It sits behind us right now in this window," he waved. "And every day we work in its shadow, in a very literal sense. It has come to mean something to us as well, and when we launched our new campaign, we saw it as a strong symbol of safety and stability. And–"

"And so you used the Holy Mountain of the Sky in the service of your greed!" the druid interrupted.

"Hee-oo-ARR!" both his companions chanted again.

"Yes," admitted Heiermach without hesitation. "We did. And we are sorry for it. Our marketing department made a terrible mistake in our ignorance."

"So why have you brought me here?" the druid asked. "Do you seek to receive forgiveness for your blasphemy against the Holy Mountain?"

Heiermach nodded. "Yes, that is my intention. We will be issuing a formal apology but I wanted to personally apologize to you first. When we spoke on the phone, you told me that you recognized our ignorance and our lack of intention to cause offense. Well, we are no longer ignorant. And DVG would like to not only apologize, but to offer something more—something tangible, as a symbol of our repentance."

"You understand that what you would call tangible is not the true reality behind the universe," the druid said.

"I'm sure you'd know much more about that than me," said Heiermach. "And I am pleased to defer to your expertise on the matter. But according to what we've learned of the financial state of your organization, most of your members have not yet entirely escaped the need to utilize certain elements of the tangible world."

The druid raised an eyebrow.

"If I may say so without causing offense, your temple rebuilding fund isn't exactly flush with cash. And the temple is in some need of repairs that your organization cannot presently afford. I have also been advised that the repair of the temple has been deemed desirable for both religious and tourism-related reasons."

"What are you offering?" the druid said, his eyes narrow with calculation. Or possibly suspicion, it was hard to read the old man.

"I have already authorized our marketing department to make a substantial donation."

"How substantial?"

"DVG is willing to fund the temple's complete refurbishment," Heiermach said.

"The Temple of the Sky is ancient, businessman," said the druid. "It is not something you can simply remake with glass and steel. The bricks of the altar came from a stone which fell from the sky. The bricks in the walls were cast by willing slaves who knew their labor would give them wings in eternity. Do you think you can buy us off by hiring a crew of infidels to build walls of plastic and steel? With mammon you seek to rectify the evil you have committed in the name of mammon!"

Heiermach calmly pushed a tablet across the table. The druid took it.

"We merely seek to do the right thing, Chief Druid," said Heiermach. "And to demonstrate the sincerity of our apology."

The druid's face became less hard as he looked at the tablet.

"You may use these funds to hire whomever you please—no infidels need apply. Or you may disburse the funds as you see fit, to those members of your faith who wish to take part in the project," Heiermach continued. "We had three different architectural firms provide us with estimates, so we are confident that whatever method you choose, this will more than cover the cost. And this is intended as a gesture of good will, made by those who are not enemies of your faith, in order to restore good relations between us. We ask for nothing more in return."

The druid looked up. "It seems you truly are interested in our forgiveness."

"Yes," said Heiermach. "We are truly committed to mutual tolerance and acceptance. Our clients come from a wide variety of religious and philosophical backgrounds, and we were devastated to learn that we had caused such serious offense."

The druid nodded slowly. "I realize that your corporation did not know what it was doing. It is as if a child scrawled an image of his father but forgot to add the arms. The omission does not mean the child intends to dismember the father, only that his perception is deficient."

He stroked his beard and eyed the tablet again. "When will these funds be delivered?"

"If you will speak to your people and grant us permission to make a public apology, mention our donation to the rebuilding of the temple, and publicly call for an end to violence and protests, I will authorize the payment as soon you provide us with an account that is capable of receiving the funds. That could be as early as next week. If there are any difficulties, our legal team can address them in cooperation with your people."

The druid nodded. "Thank you, Chief Heiermach. I believe you are sincere and a man of your word. I will accept your offer. And I will allow you to share your repentance and your desire to make penance through funding our building project. The temple is structurally unsound, yet we have never possessed the means to properly repair it. Our faith is not a rich one as you would measure it. Our riches are primarily contained in our hearts and our future wings."

Heiermach nodded. "I am truly appreciative. And with that richness of heart in mind, do you believe your acceptance of our repentance will keep my people safe from further attacks by overzealous and misguided individuals?"

"Be careful who you call misguided," said the druid. "The gods direct men as they see fit, and I am but a vessel for their will. I will share my belief in your intentions, as well as the news of your donation, then publicly call for an end to violence. I cannot say for certain, however, that the gods themselves will be satisfied. One may yet direct one of the faithful to avenge the violation of the Holy Mountain. But I do believe the danger will be significantly reduced, as you have taken proper and fitting measures for repentance. I, for one, do forgive you."

He rose and stretched out his arms towards Heiermach, his glittering sleeves dangling like limp wings. "Go in peace and one day may you fly."

Heiermach bowed and the druid and his men swept out of the room, leaving behind the faint scent of incense. The CEO took a deep breath and looked around. "Well, I could certainly use a drink after that nonsense. Anyone else?"

We left the office with Heiermach in an armored car provided by Pinker, and wound our way through the city's wide streets as the car's AI took us back to Heiermach's house. When we arrived, we inspected his town home, examining it for bombs, bugs, and traps. It was over one hundred years old, with the recycled metal composite flooring that Heiermach informed us was all the rage at the turn of the century. Everything was tasteful and expensive and perfectly boring in that corporate executive way. The house AI was an antique, but she gave us the complete architectural plans for Heiermach's place along with the two adjoining town homes. Unlike some I've seen, they didn't share an attic or a crawlspace, but the wall access on either side bothered me.

If I were after the guy, I'd track the heat registers to establish locations, blow one of the adjoining walls to make a dynamic entrance, and clear the place. A hit team could be in and out in less than ninety seconds. That meant that in addition to night watches, whoever was on watch was going to have to be fully suited just to ensure he wasn't taken out by the entry blast. It also meant that we were going to have to track the heat registers of the neighbors, just to make sure neither they, nor any uninvited guests, were up to no good.

The back of the building looked down into an alley and over a wall into a small park with sidewalks. Ward unboxed a state-of-the-art sniffer in case there were any toxins or explosives stowed somewhere on the property. At one point he thought he'd found something, only to sigh in relief when we opened the bathroom cabinet and found a spilled container of cleaner that had gotten into some insecticide.

"Mix was getting close to old chemwar, sir," he told a relieved Heiermach. "You really should consider going organic."

"I should have gotten a better cleaning service to scrub the place before I moved in," Heiermach said. "I've never even opened that cabinet."

I secured all the windows and the back door, adding locks and sensors that would send a signal straight into our comm system if they triggered. Zelag interrogated Heiermach about his time on Feymanus to date and if he'd ever seen anything even remotely suspicious before the marketing director was knocked off. Nothing.

Jones caught me as I was installing the final heat reader in the hallway that shared a wall with the neighbor's kitchen. "This is overkill, Tommy."

"No, this is exactly what we're paid for," I said. "That crazy lady with the stunpen was about as sophisticated as a tapeworm. But we're the best, so we're going to do it by the book. DVG isn't paying for half-assed security."

"Yeah, you're right," Jones said. "By the book it is." He waved a hand at the window. "But we're going to spend a lot of time doing nothing."

I engaged the sensor and flicked my finger against the glass. Jones jumped. "Geez, Tommy. Knock it off!"

"Gets you right in the skull, don't it?"

"Yeah."

"So it works. That's good. Now we'll see what Mr. Heiermach wants us to do from here," I said. "He's busy and he's his own man—we need to give him his space without actually giving him any."

"We have to watch him shower now?"

"Assuming he's not going to let you get in there with him," I said, then evaded the knife hand he threw at my throat.

We walked down the stairs and I could hear Heiermach still talking with Zelag. "…and it's really been nice. The golf course is good, the local food is great, and the wine is all right. Plus, Shelly is going to enjoy the dog park behind the house, and…" Heiermach trailed off as we entered the room. "Well, all set?" he said.

"Yes," I said. "Nobody gets in here without us knowing it."

"Great," said Heiermach. "You guys just make yourselves at home in the downstairs here. There's a tri-D, some drinks in the fridge, and the bedroom only has a single in it, but the sofas are good."

"No problem," I said. "Thank you. We have everything we need in the vehicle. And we won't all be sleeping at once, we'll be keeping a 24-hour watch. Once you're inside here, you're pretty secure. Keep the blinds drawn, don't answer the door unless your AI ID's the guest first, even then—call us first. And don't even think of going out and wandering the neighborhood alone."

"I have a gun," Heiermach volunteered.

"I should hope so," said Jones. "Men without guns are like chicks without–"

I shushed him quickly and looked at Heiermach. "That's good. You should have a gun. However, you're not going to need it. Keep it by your bed if it makes you feel better, but remember: you have the galaxy's best and baddest warriors surrounding you. Nothing is going to happen."

"I'm sure," said Heiermach with relief. "Heck, I'd probably be safe so long as you guys were on the same continent. No worries here."

"Just precautions," I said. "We've also got your neighborhood under watch. If a cat steps into your yard, we'll see it. Ward set up a sniffer out front. Any explosives or common toxins approach within a block or so, it will pick up errant molecules and all our jacks will light up. This house is secure. But any time you go outside, we go with you."

"Great," said Heiermach. "I've got some work I'm going to do in the office upstairs. I suppose you can take care of yourselves from here on out."

I nodded.

"Wait—one more thing, Mr. Heiermach, if you don't mind" Jones said. "If you can answer just one question for us?"

"Anything."

"Where can we get a good steak?"

Now that the house was tight and Heiermach was tucked in, I decided that we could relax a bit and play Grill the New Guy, a perennial favorite of mercenaries and soldiers everywhere across the galaxy. We hadn't had much of a chance to do so en route, since we'd been occupied with learning everything we could about the DVG building, Heiermach's house, the caterpillar crazies, and arguing over our equipment requirements.

"So tell me, Zelag, I hear you're Rhysalani. Did you see any action on Bassatria?"

"Nope," Zelag said, sipping his beer.

We were sitting in Heiermach's kitchen, now fortified with seven different kinds of high class beer. We'd been moving since early morning and I was certain enough about our precautions that we'd decided to sit for a spell and catch our breath. We'd changed out of our battlesuits, though I wore a SurTac secondskin vest under my civvies and hid the Reaper inside a jacket holster.

"Rhysalan girl's swim team, then?" Jones asked Zelag.

"Warmer," said Zelag, perfectly bouncing a wedge of lime off Jones's forehead with a flick of his robotic fingers.

"Male stripper," I ventured.

"Bingo," said Zelag.

"Seriously, though," Ward said. "Marks had a reason to pick you for this one. I haven't worked with you before, and these guys haven't either. What's your background? Where have you fought?"

"Not much to tell, to be honest," Zelag said. "I was Ascendancy Navy. High Guard. Didn't see much action, though I spent all the time I could at the shooting range. I did kill a pirate once. Trafficker. He'd managed to rob one of those expensive deep sleep facilities where you can 'skip your current century in hope of a better future' or whatever. Stole three women, still in their coffins. My guess was he was planning to jack them for a brothel or something. You know how they wire those chicks up and you can get made-to-order services from them?"

We knew. I'd seen it before.

"This guy was a freak. You should have seen how he decorated his ship. It was like a flying whorehouse. I led the boarding party. I found him in the cargo bay with the coffins. He shot at us but we were suited. He wasn't and I shot back, took him out with three shots. Zap, zap, zap, game over. And that's the sum total of my combat experience."

"You joined Wardogs after that?" I asked.

Zelag laughed. "Nah, I did two full terms. That was just the extent of my combat experience. I got a high proficiency rating for dealing with people when they tested me at OCS, so I ended up in the Navy's ambassador program. I was a lieutenant, and spent most of my service on one courier ship or another, going planet to planet. 'Your Most Special Royal Highness, how may I hold your hand?' 'Mr. Planetary President, here's how you access the ship's library.'"

Jones flipped a packet of hot sauce at him and Zelag caught it, again with his robotic arm. "I guess I'm just good with people," he said, pinching the packet between metal fingers and squeezing a bright stream of orange back towards Jones.

"A diplomat," Ward said. "I guess that's why corporate wanted you on the team. Makes sense. We had enough ass-kickers, so they figured we needed an ass-kisser to keep us from ruffling the native feathers."

"How did you lose the arm?" Jones said, wiping sauce off his shirt. "You wipe the wrong royal arse or something?"

Zelag shrugged. "Something like that. So I went out and bought this one."

"Not in action, I take it," I said.

Zelag shrugged again. "There are different kinds of action. Hey, you guys did the Ulixis thing. Did it really happen the way they all say?"

"Which part?" Ward said, frowning.

"Scuttlebutt says Captain Marks nuked a whole damn royal family and their guard," Zelag said, leaning in and speaking so he wouldn't be overheard.

Ward shrugged and smiled a little. Jones whistled innocently.

"But it's true, right? How do you get away with that sort of thing?" Zelag said.

"You should know, diplomat. Diplomacy by other means," Jones said.

"So he really did it? He set off a nuke?" Zelag pressed.

We refused to confirm or deny the accusation, but our silence, combined with our expressions, was obviously enough confirmation for him.

"My God, he really did it," Zelag exclaimed. "That's crazy."

Jones relented a little and laughed. "Marks isn't crazy, but he is a stone-cold bastard. Frozen stone-cold! But talking about crazy, how about that monk today? There's some real crazy. And not the good kind."

"I think he was a druid," I said. "Not a monk."

"Same difference. Anyway, he was a nutjob," Ward said.

"A greedy nutjob," Jones said. "Did you see how his high-minded principles melted away when he figured out he could get paid? I'll bet they don't even use that money to fix their stupid temple."

"They should spend it wisely," I said. "On wine, women, and designer pharmas."

"I don't think they're totally nuts," Zelag said. "I've met some that are all right. Not full druids, though. Actually, they were chicks. Met them on a hiking trip on Purumose."

"Chrysalans?" I asked.

"So they said," he said. "One of them had a butterfly tattoo across her face. Good dancer."

I shook my head. "I was raised OCC. No tattooed faces for us."

"Ah, the good old Orange Catholics," Jones laughed. "That's vintage crazy there."

"Nah," said Ward. "The OCC is pretty respectable. They're civilizing. They teach right and wrong."

"I don't know, look at Tommy," said Jones. "It clearly didn't stick."

"What do you mean?" I protested.

"Do I really need to point out how completely you have failed to grasp 'thou shalt not kill?' "

I had to admit, he had a point.

"Well, I never coveted nobody's cow," I protested lamely.

Zelag shrugged. "My sister converted to OCC. It seems to work for her. They got her off tripjacking and back into the real world again."

"Hey, whatever helps," Jones said. "But even the Universal Church of Man makes more sense than that superstitious crap."

"Of course it does," said Zelag. "That's because it's based on science."

"So you're UCM?" I asked Zelag.

He shrugged. "It makes as much sense as anything. We do good for our fellow Man, we live a life of reason, we keep the faith. Asimov was on to something. There's a reason the Ascendancy endorses the UCM instead of, say, the Zen Rastas."

"Zen Rastas are cool," Jones said. "They never cause much trouble."

"Too busy getting high," I said.

"Nothing wrong with that," Jones said.

"They are better than Raja Shiva," Ward added.

"Oh, sweet Possenti," I said. "Who isn't?"

"The universe will end in fire!" said Zelag in a deep voice. "How about we burn it now?"

"Yeah, they make the local culties seem respectable," I said. "Though I knew this one chick who said her sister was a Neo-Lakshmian hooker. You plow her and give a good donation, your fields are guaranteed to grow."

"There's a religion I can get behind," Jones said. "Literally!"

Zelag laughed. "I bet she was making that up. That sounds like Discordian levels of crazy."

"I take serious offense at that," Jones said, affecting to be wounded. "Some diplomat you are!"

"Why? Discordians just like to stir up trouble," Zelag said. "I had to escort one of their popes once. He walked into my quarters stark naked and asked me if there were any female crew members available to give him massages. With oil. He was very specific about the oil."

"All Discordians are popes," said Jones. "And maybe he had a sore back."

Zelag shrugged. "Whatever. They're whackjobs."

"Pleased to meet you," said Jones, flipping a small golden ID card towards Zelag. "That's Pope Whackjob to you, Diplomat."

Zelag picked it up and read out loud. " 'Please acknowledge the bearer of this document as Virgil Howard Jones, Most Holy Pope of the Pan-Galactic Temple of Eris Esoterica.' Well, damn! Don't that beat all!"

Jones smiled as we passed the card around in disbelief. He'd told us before, but we'd never taken him seriously.

"Jones, you planning on disrupting Wardogs?" I asked. Discordians were famous for, well, sowing discord. It's kind of their thing. And I figured it was the sort of thing that, as team leader, I should clamp down on.

"Yeah, they installed me here as part of our long-term plan to have Diplomat here give us oil rub-downs," Jones replied drily. "Besides, after Ulixis, I can truly swear that I've never seen any organization even halfway as disruptive as WDI."

He had a point. We'd dropped more nukes in the sub-sector than Raja Shiva had in years, and that was just on our last mission.

"So, what's your secret name?" Zelag asked. I had forgotten about that. Members of the Pan-Galactic Temple of Eris Esoterica were given secret names by the church. Or organization. Or whatever you want to call it.

Jones shrugged and took his card back.

"They get secret names?" Ward said.

Zelag nodded.

"Wait a minute," I said, as a memory surfaced. "I remember that joint on Faraday. The strip club. And that one dancer said she was a pope and she bowed to you before she threw her pasties in your drink."

"The Most Holy Pope Maleeya," Jones said wistfully. "Yeah, she's my kind of religion. She recognized my papacy on sight."

"That is insane," Ward said.

Jones shrugged. "At least I live by my church's teachings. That's more than any of you can say."

"You better not let that crazy get in the way of the mission," Ward said.

"Hey, I'm solid," Jones pointed out. "And you know it. There is a time and a place for everything, brother. I'm all about the mission."

"Yeah, he knows it," I said, before an argument could break out. "And speaking of time and place, we should sort out the watch schedule and whoever is first should suit up. Just in case."

"I'm good for whatever," Zelag said. "Slot me in where you need me."

You know, he was kind of a diplomat, I thought. That sort of thing might actually be useful.

"Dibs on the game console," Ward announced.

Chapter 3

Two weeks later I stood on a platform behind Chief Executive Officer (Planetary) Heiermach, suited up and carrying both my Reaper and my Popov-Norinco 60. I was glad for my battlesuit's climate control as I watched the important men and women around me sweating in the hot afternoon sun.

I'd placed Zelag and Ward down in front of the stage, behind the local fuzz. Jones was on the stage platform with me, also a bit behind Heiermach. The crowd was pretty big. I'd estimate between twenty and thirty thousand people were there. The whole thing was a legitimately big deal.

DVG and the Chrysalans had managed to put this event together and get it advertised quickly. I suppose you can do stuff like that when you have more money than God. There were plenty of locals present, along with more than a few offworld tourists, historians and media crews interested in the temple. I had no doubt I'd end up in the background of a half-dozen documentaries. Good thing I was wearing my exo and my visor was mirrored.

Wardogs had provided us with an armored luxury skycar and a driver to escort Mr. Heiermach. That got us to the mountain in about five minutes instead of driving an hour or two through the desert. Mount Xirtis looked close through the windows of DVG HQ but the flat terrain played tricks on you.

The ceremony itself was typical PR stuff. Sappy speeches by local politicians and a university professor, various religious stuff, some music, blah blah blah. At one point some young Chrysalans did a little dance with gauzy wings on their backs, then we had to listen to a guy playing some sort of glass organ with his feet. I was desperate for coffee to stay awake within the first ten minutes, and I'd been standing here for two hours.

Fortunately, our suits are well-stocked with pharma. I set it to zing me with a little chemical pick-me-up whenever I started nodding and my heart rate dropped too low.

Heiermach played emcee himself. He was good at it too. He made it look easy, introducing each person and pronouncing their names correctly, then standing back and letting them go for their allotted time, then stepping in and moving everything along to the next portion of the program if it looked as if they were going to go on too long.

"And next we have a woman who is both a priestess of the temple and an honored historian," Heiermach announced, his hand on the shoulder of a heavy, older woman with facial tattoos. "You may have seen her book on the divine origins of the temple and the many fascinating events which took place over the centuries on this very ground. Her work has been preserved in the Alexandrian national library, and she has been recognized by the Academy of the Allied Planets as a—"

A disturbance near the front, at the barriers, interrupted Heiermach. My visor was jacked into the security grid and gave me a tactical summary. Four yellows were pushing through the surveillance field and starting to scuffle with the local police. "Possible hostiles at barrier!" I yelled into my comm, but I could already see Ward and Zelag converging rapidly on the scrum, so I held my position. Just to be safe, I pulled my Reaper and stepped in front of the CEO and the confused historian, holding it up so no one would think I was aiming it at them. Jones stood behind Heiermach, facing backwards in case a second threat materialized from behind the stage.

I focused on the four men and confirmed they were hostiles. They were dressed like tourists, but they were armed with vibro blades and had put the police down fast. Two officers already lay bleeding on the ground, while a third was staggering away holding his bleeding stomach. I flicked the Blitz to a moderate dispersion and braced to fire, but before I had the chance there were multiple flashes of plasma fire from both flanks and all four of the attackers went down hard.

The crowd was yelling and shouting and starting to get frantic.

"Tell them the threat is neutralized!" I said to Heiermach. "Keep them from rioting!"

He recovered fast, taking the mic. "Ladies and gentlemen—everything is under control. Please remain calm—please stay where you are!"

"Jones, stay with Heiermach," I ordered, then jumped down off the stage.

On the ground were four men, two of them neatly burned through center mass by plasma bolts. Ward and Zelag were already there.

"Ward, Zelag? Who torched these two?" I asked.

"That was me," Zelag admitted. "I nailed them with my Cerebus."

"Good shooting," I said. "Though non-lethal would have been better."

I kicked myself mentally. I should have specified that to the team. We wanted captures, not kills. Assuming knowledge was not good leadership, especially since Zelag was a new guy.

"I didn't kill mine," Ward said, pointing to the other bodies on the ground. They were still breathing with no burns. Stunned. One of them had lost his hair—a wig? I looked at his detached hair, then at his head. On it was a network of green tattoos, ending at his face where they'd been obscured by makeup. I pulled at the other guy's hair and it came off as well, also revealing ink.

Then I examined the other two. All of them were wearing wigs. They must be radical monks who hadn't gotten the memo. Apparently the druid was right and not everyone was easily convinced of DVG's contrition. Or maybe the gods were still pissed.

One of the two wounded police officers was now sitting up, his arm slashed from elbow to shoulder. The other one was being carried off on a stretcher.

"Damn Chrysalans," said the local police chief, taking my arm and addressing me over the murmur of the crowd. I nodded. He shook his head. "I swear, I know they've been around a long time, but if I had my druthers…"

We'd introduced ourselves to the chief before the event when discussing the security plans and he'd told me in no uncertain terms what he thought of the "crazy cultists and their stupid temple." I watched the police search the living and the dead. All four of the faux tourists had been carrying blades. I thanked Ares none of them had been wearing an explosive vest. *Though the sniffers would have picked that up*, I mused. *Okay, a disrupter. Thank Ares none of them had a disrupter.*

"You'd better make an announcement," I said to the police chief, aware that the crowd was restless. "Get this thing back on track."

I took the stage again, as did the police chief. He made a quick announcement, stating that two police officers had been injured in the line of duty but were receiving care and that "security had neutralized the threat and we shouldn't let terror derail this momentous occasion." The event resumed, with Heiermach thanking the universe, the Chrysalan gods, and the sacred mountain for keeping everyone safe. We made it through without incident. As the sun set over the temple, the chief druid took the stage and publicly hugged Heiermach, accepting his repentance and blessing him for it, then sharing a drink from a large and glittering ceremonial chalice. It was passed around on stage among a circle of Chrysalans along with important members of the city and the DVG staff, then torches were lit and songs were sung for another half hour before the event came to a close.

And that's when everything went rodeo.

Heiermach and three other DVG execs joined us in the skycar after saying some fond farewells to their newly minted cultist friends. Just after we took off, their Director of Sales came out with a bottle of champagne and popped the cork, then passed out some paper cups. They offered us some but we shook our heads.

"Just a little for me," Heiermach said. "I'm feeling really tired all of a sudden."

"Probably stress," the sales director said, pouring him a half glass. "You did a great job up there. Makes me proud you're my boss." The execs clinked glasses. "To success!" one of them said, then they each took a swig of the champagne.

"What's the matter, boss?" the salesman asked.

Heiermach set down his champagne, his hand shaking. He grimaced as if swallowing broken glass. His face was noticeably pale in the artificial light of the ship's interior.

"Mr. Heiermach," I said. "Are you okay? Would you like to lay down?"

"No," he said, "I just… oh god…"

He clutched at his stomach and winced. "Oh god, I feel like something is ripping."

His skin was turning green. The salesman looked alarmed and the sole woman on board—the same blonde I'd seen in the conference room—took his wrist.

"His pulse is racing," she said, then let go in shock. There was blood on her fingers. His wrist had peeled open where she'd touched it. "Oh god," she said. "I used to be a nurse and I've never seen anything like that."

Heiermach suddenly jerked forwards and vomited explosively onto the floor, first chunks of food and fluid, followed by a crimson gush of blood. His skin split in more places. He curled sideways in his seat, burbling incoherently and choking.

"Driver!" I yelled. "Get us to a hospital—now!"

The car spun and accelerated through the air as Heiermach jerked and shuddered.

"The champagne!" said the salesman in horror, throwing his empty cup on the floor. "It's poisoned!"

Lesions erupted on Heiermach's skin, bubbling and boiling as if they were volcanic.

"It can't be the champagne," Zelag said. "You all drank it."

Hairmach thrashed and burbled in his throat. Ward went to put a steadying hand on the sick man.

"No, Ward!" I said. "Don't touch him. Whatever he has might kill you too." I saw the nurse look at her bloody fingers in sudden fear. None of us knew what to do except get him to the hospital.

To my left, Jones popped up his visor and vomited onto the floor.

"He's dying too!" a man yelled. I looked at Jones and he made a face and shook his head. He just had a weak stomach.

The smell of the skycar was horrible. As I watched, Heiermach jerked violently and let out a final rattling exhalation. His skin looked like chewed pizza, face almost unrecognizable. Fluids soaked through his white dress shirt.

"Sweet mother of God, he's dead," the salesman whispered, pulling out a string of beads and fingering them. "Our Father, who art in Heaven…" He kept mumbling prayers as we landed at the city hospital and nurses boarded with a stretcher to carry away the mortal remains of his boss.

The whole incident had taken less than five minutes from downing the champagne to the final death rattle. I had never seen anything like it and I wondered if we were all dead men walking. I've seen some horrific stuff in my time, but this was a new level of awful.

A few moments after the hospital staff arrived, a special team in full protective gear took us in for tests. They were followed by the police, who took us in for what they described as protective custody.

Screw that, I know when I'm being arrested.

Chapter 4

I'm not ashamed to admit that I spent the next few hours almost sick with terror. I imagined I could feel things crawling around in my stomach and I wondered if my skin was going to break out in boils. After a few hours of nothing happening, I finally started to relax. The biowarfare response unit stuck us in a big clear room, stripped us naked, drew blood, swabbed our throats, flooded us with UV, dipped us in cold purple water, then in a hot yellow bath that stung our skin, and finally pronounced us clean.

Then the police wanted their turn with us. After hours of stress, both physical and mental, we weren't in very good shape to answer their questions. Which, from the police perspective, was just how they wanted us.

We answered their questions for over an hour. Did we see anyone suspicious? When were we hired by DVG? Who poured the champagne? All the typical stuff. I understood they were just doing their jobs, but the tone got more and more accusatory over the course of the morning. We'd been up all night and now this. For some reason, the police interrogator really zoomed in on Ward. I didn't know where Zelag and Jones were, but the interrogator had decided to question Ward and I at the same time.

"Are you not a mercenary?" the interrogator asked, learning into Ward's face. "Is it not possible that someone simply paid you more than you are currently receiving from your position as—how did the dossier put it—a 'security professional?'"

Ward exploded, jumping up and shoving the officer backwards.

"Who the hell do you think you are?" he yelled. "Goddam it, you don't ever talk to no Wardog like that!"

"Ward!" I snapped. "Sit down!"

"I've had enough sitting," he said, holding the officer up off the ground by the front of his shirt. "This stupid pig has–"

He was cut off mid-sentence as another cop took him down with one of those obnoxious KareMore police stunners. To their credit, they didn't let him fall hard as he crumpled to the floor. They caught him, cuffed him, and carried from the room right away.

"That was completely unnecessary," I said to the interrogator as the man straightened his collar. "Look, it's the morning after we witnessed our client die horribly and now you're treating us like we did it. Cut him some slack."

"You'll have to talk to the judges about that," the man huffed. "Your buddy just assaulted an officer of the law. He's under arrest and you will be as well unless you cooperate. Maybe you would like to give us some better answers, Thomas?" he said, taking a seat across from me.

"I've given you answers," I said. "You know my background, my job here on Feymanus, my knowledge of Mr. Heiermach—I'm not sure what else you want."

"Tell me about your team," the interrogator asked. "How well do you know your men?"

I sighed. Fragging paper-pushers. Maybe a few more answers would get him off my back. "Quite well," I answered.

"Tell us about Virgil Jones."

"Jones is a good guy. I always thought he was real serious, then I got to know him better. He's somewhat of a joker underneath. Good-natured. He's a fine soldier, very cool under fire."

"Is he religious?"

I frowned. "Not exactly." I figured this was not the time to reveal his papacy.

"Does he smoke?"

"I haven't seen him," I said. "Actually, yeah. A cigar, once."

"Does he collect guns?"

"Come on," I said. "I'm not his mother."

The interrogator nodded slightly. "Tell me more about the man we just removed. Michael Ward."

"Ward? Ward can be a hot-head sometimes. But he's a good man and very loyal. Dependable. You question his integrity, he gets pissed. He also tends to overthink things sometimes."

"Does he have a history of violence?"

I tried unsuccessfully to suppress a snort.

"Is there something funny?"

I shook my head. "No. No, no 'history of violence,' at least not as you mean it."

"What about Jack Zelag?" the interrogator asked.

"Zelag I don't know as well," I admitted. "So far he's been solid. Ex-Navy officer, Ascendancy, not planetary. Got a diplomatic background."

"Is it true he gunned down two men at the ceremony yesterday afternoon?"

"That was my fault," I said.

"How so?"

"I failed to specify the use of non-lethal force. But his mistake was understandable. The attackers were armed and heading for the stage. And they had already broken through the police line."

"And so he immediately to lethal force?" the interrogator pressed. "That wasn't very diplomatic."

I may have snorted again at this point. The cop was getting on my nerves. "Did you miss the fact they were armed with deadly weapons and rushing the stage, after nearly killing three of your fellow officers of the law?"

"This is under investigation," the interrogator said with a shrug. "You must understand that we are looking at all angles and the fact that the four of you are non-residents and recent arrivals makes you obvious suspects in the victim's death. You were literally sleeping in

Mr. Heiermach's home, after all. Obviously, that makes you persons of interest."

"I shouldn't be," I said. "None of us should be. Wardogs is well-known for honoring contracts. And there is absolutely no motive. You pushed Ward over the top with these interrogations."

"Perhaps your organization should teach you better manners," the interrogator said blandly. "And perhaps you should take care to better prepare your team in the future. By your own admission, you failed to give them proper instructions."

"What?" I snapped. "Look, we did not screw it up! We stopped the attack, just like we were paid to!"

"Your client is dead and you say you didn't make any mistakes, yet you wish us to simply take your word that neither your nor anyone on your team is connected to the death we are currently investigating?"

I was getting cornered and I could feel it. "Look," I said. "Wardogs Inc. vets people carefully. They have a big process, lots of paperwork and physicals and everything." This was lame and I knew it, but I pressed on. I was at my limit. "So if they say they're okay, I say they're okay and you should as well."

"We don't recognize your employer as having any jurisdiction here," said the interrogator. "Unlike some of the places you may frequent, we are a nation of laws, maintained by peace officers, not hired killers."

"And your laws say I don't have to stick around all night answering questions if I'm not charged with a crime," I said. "I've cooperated and I've answered more than enough questions for now. Unless I'm under arrest, under both local and interplanetary law you need to let me walk out of here. The same goes for Zelag and Jones, unless you've stunned them like you did Ward."

The interrogator nodded to another officer who walked over and handed him my ID card. The interrogator handed it back to me.

"You may go. Please do not attempt to leave the planet. You may not return to Heiermach's residence. Your personal effects there are now part of an investigation for now. They will be released to you later if we see fit to do so. You are being observed and are asked not to leave the city. Follow Officer Tetley downstairs and he will re-unite you with your friends, with the exception of the one who assaulted me." He stood, not offering his hand.

"What about my sidearm?" I asked, standing. I'd been relieved of the Reaper at the hospital.

"Evidence," the interrogator said, then waved me off.

I was fuming but didn't want to share Ward's fate. Officer Tetley nodded to me and I followed him to the lift and down into the lobby area.

"They kept you a long time, Tommy," Jones said as I stepped off the lift. "Where's Ward?"

"Let's go," I said, flicking my eyes towards Tetley. "We'll talk later."

Tetley left us at the front door and we stepped onto the sidewalk in front of the police station. It was mid-morning, I was exhausted and we were one man short, not to mention our client had bit the dust in the worst way possible. I felt like kicking some cops around, blowing up the police station, then drinking a bottle of vodka and taking up smoking.

"Let's get some grub," Jones said. I agreed. A few blocks from the station we found a gaudily decorated diner. Other than a single customer sitting near the front, the place was ours. A server bot welcomed us and brought us to a table. This must be a cheaper joint, I mused, considering that most places here were staffed with humans. Though I was more comfortable without them. I smelled coffee and was reminded it had been way too long since my last fix.

"So," Jones asked, punching in his order on the table computer. "Where the hell is Ward?"

"Arrested," I said, taking a coffee from the robowaitress. One sugar, one cream. I considered adding a shot of bourbon as well, but decided against it.

"Arrested?" Zelag and Jones said simultaneously.

"Yeah," I said, selecting my own order. Pancakes. A double stack.

"Why?" Jones asked.

"The cops pushed him, questioned his integrity, almost accused him of doing it himself," I said. "Damned pigs."

"And he blew up," Jones said.

"Bingo. They kept pressing him until he snapped and shoved the cop. So, they stunned him and dragged him off to the tank."

"That's bullshit," Zelag said. "They should be talking to the crazy butterfly people, not us."

"What did you do?" Jones asked.

The robowaitress approached and brought my pancakes, along with Jones's and Welag's orders. She refilled my coffee silently, then wheeled off.

"Nothing. What was I supposed to do?" I said. "He was out of control and it wasn't like I could take them all down and carry him out. I did the responsible thing. I answered their questions like a good little sheep. But they had it in for Ward. They pushed him too far."

"We should bust him out," Zelag said.

"What?" I said. "You barely know him."

"He's a Wardog," Zelag said. "That's good enough for me."

"He's right, Tommy," Jones said. "We could bust him out easy."

"We're going to requisition arms from the Wardogs office so we can hit a local police station?" I said. "They've probably already cleared out everything we've got at the house and in the car."

"Naw," said Jones. "Hell, we could probably neutralize everyone in the station if I could get ahold of a few ingredients at a hardware store. Jam the sensors and the sniffers, kill the lights, hack the ventilation and put down the cops—with our optics we could get in and out in the dark—10 minutes."

"I'm not going to say I'm not tempted," I said. And I was. I'd love to put the jackasses in their place. "We'd never get off planet after that, though," I said, realizing how screwed we'd be without official Wardogs support.

"I have friends in the diplomatic corps here," Zelag said. "I could get a system jumper lined up. They wouldn't even have to know we were Wardogs. No questions asked."

I chewed thoughtfully. We could do it. Ward was our boy. If I could simply–

Then my transceiver pinged and I twitched my eyes to bring up an incoming message. I saw Jones and Zelag were receiving as well. We'd all been jacked before this mission, since the tech level allowed it.

I read the message off the table top in front of me. It wasn't really on the table, of course, but that's how it looks when you're jacked. I wasn't on AI and I was firewalled so those Unity bastards couldn't turn me Manchurian, but it was good to forgo carrying a tablet when you're in the field.

Falkland, Jones, Zelag—why the hell are you screwing around with the local police? Shut the hell up and let legal team play dice. Do not answer any more questions and for God's sake don't do anything else stupid. Client dead, lethal force utilized at public event, and now Ward is assaulting peace officers? Shut down and sit tight, the cavalry is on the way. This is NOT the time to go off the chain!

—Captain Arden Williams, Sales Division

"Damn," Jones said after I showed it to them.

"Yeah," I said. This should have been simple. Now I was in the sauce.

Zelag yawned. "I figure getting some sleep is probably the best way to keep out of trouble." He stabbed at a last piece of sausage and washed it down with a swallow of tomato juice. Or maybe it was a Bloody Mary. I didn't ask.

"Agreed," Jones said. His eyes unfocused for a moment. "There's a hotel about five minutes walk from here. Anyone got any money?"

"I have the company card," I said. I was half-way through my pancakes but I'd lost my appetite. "Let's go."

We got ourselves rooms and I lay down on the bed without undressing. I was beat inside and out.

The door chimed cheerfully, waking me up. I rolled out of bed quickly and looked for my gun, then realized it was gone. The events of the last 24 hours raced back to me. That death—geez—I tried to tell myself it was a nightmare but knew full well it wasn't. No nightmare was that vivid. I walked to the door and looked at the small security monitor to see who was outside. There I saw a pair of women and three guys in suits. The woman in front rang the chime again.

Great. Ambulance chasers. I ran my fingers through my hair and opened the door.

"Tommy Falkland?" said the woman. I nodded. "Veronique Parey. I'm a Senior Investigator in the Intelligence Department." Ah, so this was the cavalry. Not bad. "This is my partner, Bettina Wolfsganger," she continued, gesturing to the second woman. Veronique was maybe 35, tall, thin and athletic, with high cheekbones and long black hair. Bettina was a little shorter and more compact, with blonde hair and wide-set silver eyes. She was either wearing fancy contacts or had optical implants. My bet was on the latter, given her occupation.

"May we come in?" Parey asked.

"Sure," I said. "Who are these guys?" I asked, gesturing towards the guys in suits.

"Just the local element of your new legal team. Jeston, Forman, and Ashbach."

"Let me get some coffee started," I said. I walked to the small kitchenette and studied the machine I knew could produce caffeine. It had too many options and my eyes were blurry.

"Here," Wolfsganger said, walking in behind me and pressing a button. There was a hiss and a moment later a panel opened containing a mug of black coffee. "Cream? Sugar?" she said. "One of each," I replied. She pressed a couple of buttons and my coffee was complete.

"Thanks," I said, taking a sip.

"The situation is not ideal," Parey said, sitting on the edge of the bed. Two of the lawyers sat on the love seat, another stood uncomfortably against the wall. "But I've seen worse."

"Tell me about it," I said. I was starting to feel less stupid as the caffeine hit my system.

"We're working on getting Ward out," she said. There was another chime at the door and I got up to let in Jones and Zelag.

"Looks like a great party," Jones said, smiling and sitting on the bed next to Parey. "Who are you all?"

"This is our legal team, I think," I said.

Wolfsganger stood just inside the kitchenette, silently watching us over a cup of steaming tea. Zelag looked around for a seat, then sat on the bed on the other side of Parey. I stayed standing.

"We're considerably more than that," Parey said. "You and the rest of your team not only blew the mission, but managed to get yourselves into a legal mess. If you're lucky, we'll get you safely disentangled and off the planet before you screw up anything else. And while these three gentlemen are the legal team. Betti and I are investigators who have been assigned to this case. We're going to find out what happened and how they managed to get past you boys."

"We didn't kill him, you know," Zelag said.

"Of course not," Parey agreed, with a professional smile. "But let me take a little stab in the dark here. The four of you don't think much of the local police, and after you were all taken into custody, you were less than perfectly cooperative during the interview process. I'll even bet that the three of you are already planning to break into the police station and exfil Mr. Ward."

Zelag's eyes widened. Jones shrugged. I did my best to look as if the thought hadn't even crossed our minds.

"Look," she said. "I get it. You're mercs. Your job is to break stuff and do bad things. But what you have to understand is that our job is to fix things and correct the problems that are occasionally caused by excessively violent men."

"The three of you are going to have to trust us," Wolfsganger declared, entering the conversation for the first time. "This is far from the worst situation we've had to clean up. All we need you guys to do is not dig the hole any deeper, all right?"

"Thanks, Betti," Parey said, then turned back to us. "Now listen. As the first order of business, you three need to stay put, sit tight, and shut up. That is an order!"

"Who put you in charge," Jones muttered. I kicked his shin.

"The legal team will take care of the legal issues," Parey said, ignoring him. "Do not speak with the police. Do not speak with the media. Do not answer calls from Datacon Verlag or anyone else besides the five of us and Captain Williams. I'll say this again just so we are perfectly clear: you absolutely have to sit tight and shut up! Don't worry about Mr. Ward, we should have him out later today."

"He's in for assault, you know," I pointed out. "Assaulting a cop. They don't take that lightly here."

"Mr. Ward was distraught, exhausted, and inappropriately treated in an abusive manner by local law enforcement," Forman broke in briskly. "He was an innocent witness, who was discriminated against due to his alien non-resident status and his former military service, and was wrongfully accused of lying before being threatened by an overzealous interrogator. Here we have a man who served his client and performed his responsibilities to the best of his professional abilities, was twice subjected to violent trauma, did his best to save a dying man, then was deprived of sleep before being interrogated extensively by the police."

"Sounds outrageous when you put it that way," I said. "You're good."

"We only retain the best," Parey said. "And fortunately, Mr. Ward didn't actually harm the policeman."

"No blood, no charges," Ashbach added. "As a general rule."

"So you were sent here to get us off the hook?" Jones said.

"That's our immediate priority. They'll handle most of that," Parey said, nodding towards the lawyers. "However, this is no longer a corporate contract. Now it's a criminal investigation. Heiermach was almost certainly murdered by someone who had it in for Datacon Verlag. Wardogs doesn't take it lightly when one of their clients is killed. We will get to the bottom of it and make sure those responsible are brought to justice. Our reputation depends upon it."

Parey stood up, as did the lawyers.

"We have work to do," she said. "We're off to OCME. Can your jack link me?"

I nodded and we linked. Now she lit up as a friendly in my retinal display. I also could tell where she was, so long as she didn't unlink us. Parey reached in a slim black purse and pulled out a datachip and handed it to me. "This is for you gentlemen. It came in from Kantillon via C-ship." She motioned to one of the lawyers who handed me a medium-sized case. "This is yours as well. But don't go getting any ideas or looking for trouble. Clear?"

"Clear," I confirmed as they filed out. I scanned the chip on the Tri-D and an image of Captain Marks in his office appeared on the screen.

"Greetings from HQ, men. As you've learned by now, we sent a pair of investigators to figure out what happened. Betti and Vero are the real deal and they're on your side. They are serious data sharks and very resourceful. Don't beat yourselves up over the hit. I have no doubt you did the best you could. We don't win them all. We'll get you out. Obviously, the DVG contract is concluded. For now, your job is to protect Bettina and Veronique as they investigate. If anything happens to them, it had damn well better happen over your dead and dismembered corpses. They have field experience and they know what they're doing, but don't let them get in over their heads. Word is this cult may be bad news. Continue to report directly to Williams. Good luck, gentlemen."

The screen went blank.

"I guess we'd better follow them," I said, popping open the case. To my great satisfaction, it contained our sidearms, plus extra magazines, three SecondSkin suits, three official Wardogs jumpsuits, plus two sets of civvie clothes for each of us—in the correct sizes—and a bottle of bourbon. I strapped my Reaper back on with satisfaction.

Jones grinned. "I like these girls already."

"I dunno," I said. "I doubt these 'serious data sharks' had the time to go clothes shopping for three grunts. And they don't seem like the bourbon type."

"You're right," Zelag said, picking up the bottle. "Says it's from Pinker. He sends his condolences. I have to say, I feel like I misjudged the guy."

"We'll drink to him, just don't open it now," I said. "Gear up. We're heading out. Actually, where was Parey going?"

"Some place called Ockme?" Jones said, sounding puzzled.

"The Office of the Chief Medical Examiner," Zelag explained.

I looked at the bottle of bourbon. "With any luck, we'll share this with Ward tonight."

"Maybe I'll share it with Parey and Wolfen-whatever," Jones said.

"I think we're in enough trouble, Jones. Besides, they're too old for you."

"And too smart," Zelag added.

"Come on, they're both pretty hot. And that blonde is fit, too. I'll bet she does free weights."

"Jones, if you can't see that you're in over your head, you deserve exactly what you'll get from them. Anyhow, do I have to remind you of the WDI harassment policy?"

Jones laughed. "Right. On second thought, I'll share them with Ward."

"Good man."

Chapter 5

The three of us stood together in the OCME parking lot waiting for Parey to respond to my call. I noticed a security guard standing by the wall, obviously trying to decide if he should approach or not. I shook my head at him and he put up his hands and nodded. Good puppy. Unlike the police, he recognized a bigger dog when he saw one.

I called Parey a second time. She picked up after a short delay.

"Hey Parey," I said. "This is Falkland. We need to get upstairs."

"Falkland?" she said. "What are you doing here? I told you to stay put and shut up!"

"Let's just say you've acquired a personal bodyguard for the duration of your investigation," I replied. "Four of them, but you have to share with your partner."

"I appreciate your concern, Falkland," Parey said. "However, I'm quite capable of taking care of myself."

"It's not my call," I replied. "We received orders from HQ. You need to see what you can do about getting us upstairs."

"Fine," she said after a moment. "Give me a few." The line went dead.

A man and a woman in work attire ducked past us rapidly and entered the front of the building, casting furtive glances at us.

I looked around the parking lot and surrounding buildings, examining all the places where one could place a sniper.

"Excuse me?" came a tentative voice from the door. A young woman stood there with a name tag around her neck. Amy. "Are you the... um... Wardogs?"

"That would be us, Amy," Jones said with a smile, and the girl stepped back in alarm.

"Yes, we're from Wardogs, Inc.," I quickly intervened. "I assume you're here to escort us upstairs."

The girl nodded rapidly and waved us in. She quietly handed each of us an ID badge on a lanyard classifying us as "private security," then took us up to the 17th floor.

We entered a large open space. A window in front of us commanded a view over the orchards and plains outside the city. I noticed the view faced away from the mountain. Fine by me. I didn't care if I ever saw that stupid mountain again. I had assumed the medical examiner's would be a big lab, not some sort of office building. Despite the view, this office wasn't anywhere nearly as prosperous in appearance as the DVG headquarters. The colors were dingy and everything was just a bit run down. Various notices were displayed here and there. The joint had the distinct feel of government.

A few people looked up from their desks as we entered. Amy led us to a corner where Parey and Wolfsganger were sharing a small L-shaped workspace. "Where do they keep the stiffs?" Jones said under his breath.

"Dunno," I replied. "Doesn't look like a morgue to me."

"It's not," Parey said, scanning through documents on her tablet. "Bodies go to a separate facility. The data is analyzed here, however. We made an arrangement with the local government. They even gave us this spacious desk," she said, waving at the small workspace. "Not important, though. We're jacked into the city system and Wolfsganger is going through the autopsy report right now. Now go sit somewhere and don't interfere, or so help me I will turn you over to local law enforcement."

"Yes ma'am," I replied, then found a seat along the window with Jones and Zelag. I noticed Wolfsganger hadn't even noticed our presence. She had the look of a woman in deep communion with an AI. Her lips moved as she subvocalized commands, while glancing at a screen where I assumed data was being displayed.

"That girl is not all there," Zelag commented, looking at Wolfsganger.

"No," I replied. I felt a slight pang as I thought of Four-Eyes.

"I think we're gonna spend a lot of time sitting," Jones said.

"Yeah," Zelag replied. "Good chance to chill."

I watched him unsnap the armor on his cyborg arm, then tap a few spots. He sighed and lean back against the wall.

"Damn, Zelag," Jones said. "Are you doing drugs?"

"No. Listening to music."

"On your arm?" I said.

"Sure. Check it out—I can do external as well."

He blinked his left eye hard and suddenly we were enveloped in the sound of chanting over a thumping breakbeat.

"Goddammit!" Parey snapped. "What did I tell you?"

The music ceased as suddenly as it had started. Jones snickered.

"Come on," I said, standing up. "Let's give the ladies some space."

"No," said Wolfsganger unexpectedly, blinking and looking at us for the first time. "Wait a moment."

"Yes?" I said.

"Heiermach. How fast?"

"How fast was what?"

"How fast did he die once he showed symptoms?"

"Minutes," I said.

"And according to the report you gave the police, 'his skin erupted like a volcano and he vomited blood like a damn fountain?' "

"Yes."

"…'and his face looked like a chewed pizza.' "

"Right."

"Salamander," she said.

"What do you mean, Betti?" Parey asked before I could say anything.

"He was killed with a natural toxin extracted from a salamander," Wolfsgang said. She flipped her screen down and set it to Tri-D. The holographic image of a blue salamander appeared over her desk.

"Kind of cute," Jones said.

"Don't ever pet one," she said.

"Are they from here?" I asked.

"No," she said. "They are from Achernar. *Exo-Ambystoma perhorridus*. Quite rare."

"Achernar?" I said.

"The planet of the blue women," Jones whispered.

"I know," I said. Blue like the salamander. But apparently less poisonous.

"Even the victim's blood could have killed you," Wolfsganger continued. "Good thing you didn't touch him."

"The woman in the skycar did," Zelag said.

"She got blood on her skin?" Wolfsganger said, fixing him with her strange silvery stare.

"Yes, absolutely," Zelag confirmed.

"We saw her," Jones said as I nodded in agreement.

"The toxin is highly transdermal," Wolfsganger said. "That woman should have died, then. But there are no reports of any other related deaths, except the two assassins you guys shot."

Her eyes darted about, then she spoke again. "The toxin in extremely tiny doses has been used as a recreational hallucinogen. It causes some nasty side effects as well—degradation of mental capacity, paranoia, cracked skin, etc. There are also cases of individuals with partial immunity, but that takes a very unfortunate genetic mutation. No one outside Archenar should be immune. She wasn't wearing gloves?"

"No," I said. "She felt for his pulse and when she pulled her hand away it was definitely bloody."

“Did she react strangely afterward?” Wolfsganger said.

“Well, she was freaking out because her boss was vomiting blood and his skin was bubbling like water about to boil,” I said. “Other than that, though, no. She wasn’t panicking or seeing things or trying to talk to people who weren’t there.”

“Perhaps I have the wrong toxin,” said Wolfsganger, pulling her screen back up and causing the salamander to vanish. “But it fits perfectly….”

“Betti, maybe it’s still the right toxin,” Parey mused.

“How so?” said Wolfsganger.

“If there are people who have an immunity to it, could it not work in the opposite fashion? Couldn’t someone be made susceptible to a variant?”

“A targeted poison?” I said.

“Yeah,” said Wolfsganger. “DNA-coded. Of course.”

Her eyes went blank as she worked with her AI. A few moments later she refocused on Parey. “You were right. Blood samples show the toxin was uniquely keyed to his DNA. Multiple markers. Professional. Expert, even.”

“Who would do that?” Zelag said.

“Who has a motive?” Parey asked him.

He thought about it for a second, then spoke. “It has to be the Chrysalans.”

“No, not necessarily,” she contradicted him. “I would think a corporate rival would be much more likely, considering the probable expense involved.”

“I don’t believe it was the cultists,” I said. “The attack with the wigs and the vibroblades wasn’t sophisticated or expensive.”

“They were the distraction,” Zelag argued.

“They do have some ex-scientists in their midst,” said Wolfsganger. “Elsie is already pulling a list.”

“Look for any with backgrounds in DNA or chemical weapons,” Parcy said.

"Nothing public," Wolfsganger said. "Want me to have Elsie crack into the temple?"

"By all means," said Parey. "But I don't want a link back to this office."

"Of course," said Wolfsganger, her eyes already a thousand klicks away.

"Who's Elsie?" Zelag asked.

"Her augment."

We waited in silence for about a hectasec, then Wolfsganger spoke up.

"We're in. We have 44 active members who were former scientists. One member who worked in DNA therapy and chromosome regeneration. Another coded custom clones for rich clients. Yet another worked as a contractor for the military developing high-grade toxins."

"We need to talk to them," Parey mused. "It's certainly one of those three—or even all of them." She turned to me. "Are you boys up to picking them up for a little Q-and-A session?"

"Certainly."

"Ward would be helpful," Jones said.

"Elsie says he's being released right now," Wolfsganger said.

"Great," I said. "Give us locations on those three cultists and we'll round them up in no time." Then I remembered the captain. "Actually, though, Captain Marks said–"

"We'll be coming with you," said Parey, guessing my thought.

"Fine," I said. "But we're not supposed to let anything happen to you."

Parey smiled. "I may be a paper pusher, but I'm still a Wardog. Betti, we need names and current locations on these three.

"On it," her colleague said distantly.

By that evening we had Ward back and we had all three names and locations too. Now we just had to "bring them in for questioning," as law enforcement might put it.

According to the data Elsie had scored, Tango One was Albert "Raja" Green. 47 years old and a convert to the faith at age 32. He'd been a DNA therapist who left a lucrative job to 'pursue life's energy,' according to a public profile. Enjoys sushi, Chardonnay and Jai Alai. I had to look up Jai Alai—it's a weird old Terran game that involves hurling balls at walls at very high velocities. Parey and I went after Green while Jones and Wolfsganger went after Tango Two.

Zelag was tasked with keeping Ward company and talking him down from declaring war on the local police. We could have used the two of them, but I didn't think putting a weapon in Ward's hands tonight would be a good idea.

"They have baskets on their hands," Parey said, looking at the game. We were keeping an eye on our target—he was fifth row to the right, wearing a black cap. We were a little behind them in row seven. We'd followed Green here after Bettina monitored his house net and hacked the onboard box in his sky blue Toymo gravcycle. We just had to ask Elsie where he was and where he was going and she let us know, thanks to her hack of city surveillance. We'd waited 48 hours for this moment. Green had arranged to meet friends at this game and it was a simply matter of reaching the parking lot and watching for the red dot of his vehicle to come in, then switching to the security camera feed Elsie had projected onto our glasses. Once the limited AI of the stadium had him at the entrance, we just needed to watch and wait. I wish we could have worn battlesuits but we'd stick out like sore thumbs. At least Betti's AI gave us a serious tactical advantage.

"Forget the game, Parey. We need to make sure we can get him alone."

"Call me Vero," she said. "And I know that."

I carried my Reaper, tight beam set for stun. I also had a stunpen, loaded with an intoxicant, courtesy of the local Wardogs requisition officer. Parey had a Popov-Norinco Sonic Bobcat, the smallest weapon in their line. I could only get three fingers on one but it fit her smaller hand perfectly. They were generally considered a defensive non-lethal, but if you hit someone they went down hard. Elsie had helpfully hacked the stadium AI into seeing us as hired security so our weapons didn't ping the system when we walked. We'd held hands like a couple on a date and followed Green and his friends in from the parking lot. His friends were a man and a woman, apparently a couple since the guy had his arm around the girl and they were whispering in each other's ears during the game.

"Too bad we can't get him to drink another beer or two," I said. "That would send him on a break and I could nab him in the men's room. He's only had one so far."

"Good idea," she said, gnawing at her lip in thought. "Actually, I think we can arrange that." She keyed the tiny com in her ear. "Betti, would you send a 12-pack of beer up to our friends. Put in a fake order, whatever you have to do. Tell them they won it in a special promotion."

"Nice," I said, impressed, and Vero winked at me.

A minute later, a server bot rolled to Green's row and presented them with a 12-pack. I saw Albert and his friends shake their heads and laugh as they took it from the bot, then break into the beer and start drinking.

About a half-hour later, the girl got up and walked out, then returned. A few minutes after that, in between matches, Albert did the same as nature convinced him it was time for a break. I followed. Vero already stood against the wall near to the restroom, carrying on a conversation out loud as if she was on a call. I grinned at her as I followed our target into the kill zone. There were two other guys in the bathroom. One was closing the door to a stall, the other was at the sink. Green walked up the urinal, so I took up a position and ran my hands through my hair while keeping an eye on him in the mirror. When I saw he was done, I turned around, bumped into him and jabbed him in the arm with the stunpen. He looked at me in anger and surprise, then his eyes rolled and he lurched against me. I caught him as he flailed and muttered at me. The guy at the sink looked over at us and I shook my head at him. "Come on, Al, it's time to go, you've had way too much to drink," I said, helping him stagger out through the door. Vero met me outside, taking his other arm and directing him towards the parking lot.

"Sssgame's not over, whose you, where goin?"

"Shh," Vero said. "You're fine, just come with us."

A security guard eyed us as we walked out and tipped his hat at us. "Your buddy okay?" he said.

"Yeah, he's all right, he just had a few too many."

"Be careful," the guard said with a chuckle. "You don't want him to throw up in the car."

We folded Green into the back of our rented vehicle and took off. Tango One was down. That left two to go.

We took our poor drunken friend to a small house Bettina had secured for us at the edge of town. A vacation rental for tourists, helpfully available for rent on the net. Nice place. Had a pool, an air hockey table, and most importantly, a basement in which the table was kept. The basement had clinched the deal. We didn't even have to meet the owners, as Elsie had lined up clean backgrounds for a fictitious Mr. and Mrs. Aikman. Ward and Zelag waited at the house while Bettina and Jones went after the second guy. Kale Winters, former chemist, current outreach director for the Olympus City branch of the Sky People.

When we got there, Jones and Bettina were already there with Tango Two. They'd moved the table off to one side of the basement and replaced it with a chair on which they'd tied him.

"Cleanest grab I've ever seen," Jones said. "Bettina hacked the home AI, then we gassed him and his wife through the bedroom window, walked in the front door and walked right out with him. Didn't even wake the kids. His wife will wake up in the morning and wonder where he went."

"Kids?" I asked.

"They slept through the whole thing," Wolfsganger said. "I left a note on the AI saying he'd had an emergency call from the temple and would be back late afternoon."

We tied up Green in the basement next to the still unconscious Winters.

"One more to go," Wolfsganger said. "Karma Bhagwan."

"Where is he?" I asked.

"Elsie has him in the temple. He hasn't been outside in 48 hours."

"Monk?"

She nodded. "He lives there."

"So we bust in," I said.

"Piece of cake," Jones said. "If Betti and Elsie work their magic, we should be able to cut right through security and find him."

"Are you sure we're not going to get in serious trouble with all this hacking and kidnapping?" Ward said. "We've had good luck so far, but honestly, aren't we stretching it?"

"Too off the chain for you?" Vero said.

"Never," said Ward. "Well, maybe a bit. First of all, whatever AI Betti is using has to be totally illegal on this planet. It's only what, Tech 14? I thought you girls were supposed to be our respectable legal defense-slash-investigation team?"

Vero grinned wolfishly. "You boys don't know the half of it. Elsie isn't easily trackable and corporate isn't going to wait around for answers while the local fuzz putters. One of our clients was killed. We'll get to the bottom of it, grab the details, then leave all the data we find somewhere where the police will think their investigative AI did it on its own."

"I think I love you," Jones said.

Vero cocked an elegantly sculpted eyebrow at him as Zelag stifled a laugh.

"Shut up Jones," I said, then turned to Wolfsganger. "Alright, Betti. Tell us what you know about their security."

We hit the temple compound in the wee hours of the morning. Our last target wasn't in the ancient part of the ill-fated temple Heiermach had pledged to restore. That was more of a tourist attraction than anything else, with the main religious activity now taking place in a sprawling compound of more modern buildings that were constructed a few hundred meters from the sacred stones of the original temple. Betti stayed behind at our safe house while Vero, me, Jones, Zelag and Ward went for the temple. We suited up in full armor this time, Vero included. It took a while to get her acclimated but she insisted on coming with us so I insisted on her being in a battlesuit. She didn't think it was necessary, but we had our orders.

I had her suit up at the safe house before we went out, helping her put on the suit over her sports bra and tights, making sure everything fit properly and she was comfortable. It wasn't the worst job I'd ever had.

"Can you see us in the display?" I asked her after she locked her faceplate down.

"Blue dots," she said.

"Yes," I said. "Red will be hostiles, which means everyone else in the compound, with the exception of our target in green. He'll also have a flashing rectangle around him. Blink hard with your left eye to zoom out and see overview, then hold it shut to zoom to your location."

"Got it," she said a moment later. "I got training in a similar system a long time ago."

"No sweat," I said. "They've not likely to have weapons capable of taking you down easily. You get hit, don't panic. Just keep moving. We'll get you out safely. We won't leave anyone behind."

"Thanks," she said. "I got this. Don't worry about me."

I turned to Ward, Jones and Zelag. "She's ready as she'll ever be. You ready?"

They nodded.

The plan was to drive out along the road near the temple, checking in to a small camp site popular with hikers and pilgrims, then to head out into the woods with our packs and travel roughly two kilometers to the temple fence, break through and into the compound, then trust Bettina and Elsie to get us inside where we'd find our target and get him out. We had bulky robes we'd throw over our battlesuits but that would only disguise us a little. Our main advantage was surprise.

It was early evening when we made it to our first destination. I could feel the adrenaline in my veins as we pulled into the campground. I always got a bit nervous at the beginning of a job but it was mixed with excitement. Like jumping out of an aircraft. I smiled at the bored guy at the check-in booth and he greeted us. Above his booth, a large resin statue of a one-armed monk grinned down over the office.

"Barton," I said, giving the name we'd used for the campsite. The attendant looked in the computer and found our reservation.

"Why's the guy have one arm?" Zelag asked the man, pointing up. "Some sort of one-armed saint?"

"Naw," the attendant said. "Long time ago a guy disassembled and stole the statue in the middle of the night. The boss finally found it but it was missing an arm. Ten years later, the arm was found. Boss still hasn't gotten around to putting it back on. At this point it's a landmark, you know? He's probably never going to do it. Anyhow, you're set. Have a good time. Showers up front, open mic later tonight at the cantina. Catch me when you check out." He pointed at a spot on the map beside the booth. "You're here."

"Thanks," I said.

We rolled slowly into the campground, cruising past a few active camp sites. Most were empty, but a few campers nodded or waved as we passed. I smelled cooking food and tobacco. I saw more than one person who was obviously jacked in to some entertainment and shook my head. No one knew how to unwind anymore.

"It might be nice to go camping sometime without taking the risk of being shot," Jones commented.

"No money in it," Ward said.

We'd picked our site based on its location away from the others. It was a primitive site, hidden in a clump of thin trees and scrub brush. Most of the surrounding area was flat so I guessed someone had planted the trees long ago. Better than camping without shade.

We parked our truck so it blocked the view of us from the drive. There was no one else in sight but we could see dappled light farther up the road from other sites.

We jumped out and unloaded our packs and a pair of cheap tents. We set them up quickly to give the appearance of sticking around, then set up a few camp chairs and busted out a cooler of drinks and some sandwiches and fruit.

Ward gathered some branches and lit a fire. We could hear the sound of laughter and music coming in fitful waves from the front of the campground, carried on the breeze. I half-wished this was a real camping trip as we sat around the fire shooting off our mouths.

"You ever go camping before, Parey?" Ward asked at around midnight. The rest of the camp noises had died down and the music was done. Our fire was just embers and the night had gotten cool.

"Not my style," she said. "Give me five stars and turn-down service every time."

"No, it's fun," he said. "You drink and sit around a fire eating junk food half the night, singing songs and telling stories. The best is when you go way out. None of this campground stuff with showers and everything. You should come back from a camping trip with grime under your nails, reeking of sweat and smoke and fish guts."

"No thanks," Vero said, wrinkling her nose.

"You're not missing much," Zelag said.

"What?" said Jones. "You still mad that Bigfoot ate your arm?"

Zelag winged a crumpled-up jerky wrapper at him.

"It's about time," I said, looking at my comm display. "Suit up."

The men and I stripped down and got into our battlesuits, politely turning our backs so Vero could do the same.

"Good to have a rifle again," Jones said, taking his Popov-Norinco 60 from the trunk.

"Remember to keep it non-lethal," I warned.

"Sorry about last time," Zelag said in a rueful voice.

"Not your fault," I said. "But in general, it is considered advisable to avoid killing civilians if at all possible."

"Hey, Falkland," Vero called. "A little help with my helmet, please?"

I helped her tuck her hair into her helmet and lock it into place, then we grabbed our packs and rifles, chucked our clothes in the tents and headed off through the woods towards the temple.

The stars glittered above. Two small moons were in the sky, one full, the other a sickle. I could see the far-off glow of mining station lights on the dark portion of the sickle moon. It made for a romantic evening. And here I was with a beautiful older woman raiding a cult compound. I felt like laughing.

We reached the boundary fence in about 20 minutes. Jones cut through the thick composite grid with a laser cutter. No alarms sounded. As promised by Betti, the sensors were off. In a few minutes Jones had a nice, neat square cut out of the fence. We threw on our robes and went through, then pushed the square of composite grid back into place. Our robes blended in with the night better than our battlesuits would but they were somewhat irritating to wear.

"Eyes on," I said.

"I count 20 hostiles inside, ex Tango," Jones said.

"Civilians," Vero corrected. We ignored her.

There was a red dot about 300 meters from our position, moving around the gray grid of the closest building.

"Night watch," Ward said as the dot moved deliberately around the perimeter.

"Let him pass," I said.

We waited as he rounded the other wall and continued on his path.

The compound was mostly dark with a few plasma lights, guttering in imitation of the torches which lit the temple long ago. Further on, full rows of plasma lights lit the ancient temple, which soared up into the darkness in the rippling light. A few birds circled its spires against the velvety sky, feathers lit from below.

I zoomed out and made our target. "He's in the sleeping quarters at 1 o clock," I said, noting the green dot. It wasn't moving, which hopefully meant he was asleep. The red dots scattered here and there were mostly motionless, though a few moved slowly about inside their rooms.

"Elsie says we should go in through the kitchen," Vero said. On our HUDs it was marked with a blinking light green chevron.

"Move in," I said, and we cut quickly across through the compound's gardens into the shadow of the first building's wall.

"Second guard incoming," Zelag said as we crouched in the darkness. He was moving up the alley between this building and the next. I saw the glow of a cigarette and then saw the man was apparently just out for a walk. He was unarmed and wearing a robe much like ours. The man walked right past us, chanting quietly to himself. It looked like his cigarette was rolled by hand. I flipped off my air filter and smelled the strong herbal aroma of his smoke. Damn hippies. Once he had moved on, so did we. Jones first, then Vero, then Ward and I, then Zelag. We darted along the edge of the building first, then moved briskly past a light, then reached the edge of the dormitory, then we followed the wall around to the kitchen entrance in the back.

Someone was moving inside but not near our position. The windows were small and I hoped no one was laying awake in bed and looking out as we passed. If they did look, I hoped they'd just see some people in robes and go back to sleep. We got to the kitchen door and there was still no sign of any movement inside. I heard the door click and jumped, then realized Betti had just unlocked it for us.

We moved in and shut the door, our optics instantly adjusting to the darkness.

"Don't knock anything over," I whispered. "Through the kitchen, through the dining area, long hallway through sleeping quarters.

Tango is in eighth cell on the left. Ward, Jones, stun and retrieve. Vero, you and I will stay and secure the door here in case anyone comes through looking for a late night snack. Zelag, you secure the door leading into dining area."

"Someone's moving in the dormitory area," Jones said.

I checked my visor. "Looks like he's in a room. Don't worry about it. Go."

Outside I could see a couple of dots moving around, but they weren't anywhere near us.

The men moved out leaving Vero and I alone in the dark. Their footsteps clanked and sounded far too loud in the silence, though I knew they were being as quiet as they could. I also knew the gain and limiter built into my suit was boosting my natural hearing. My heart raced. Even through her helmet, I could hear Vero breathing beside me and almost convinced myself I could hear her heartbeat as well.

Even though the timer was displayed, I counted off the seconds in my head, trying not to count too quickly. Thirty seconds to the room. Ten seconds to stun and carry out the tango. Forty seconds back.

Now two blue dots were in the target's room. Another red dot was moving around the outside of the building again. Vero tapped me on the arm. I nodded.

Ward and Jones returned with their prize in tow. Zelag followed behind them.

I was just about to open the exterior door when I saw the red dot outside moving back towards our position.

"Tommy, someone's outside," Jones hissed unnecessarily. Bhagwan was now slung over his shoulder. "Here, Zelag, you take him for now."

Zelag shrugged and dutifully shouldered the load.

"We'll let the guy outside pass," I said. "Ten count, then we move."

Then I saw something new on my display. Someone was leaving one of the dormitory rooms. The lights in the dining area came on. I heard Vero curse under her breath. In a moment, whoever it was could reach the kitchen. Outside, the target was still moving towards the door.

"Someone's coming!" Vero said. "We have to go now!"

Then the door swung open and a silhouette appeared in the light coming out of the kitchen. I saw a surprised face in a hood, then Ward lashed out with the butt of his PN60, catching the guy in the jaw with an audible crack. He crumpled to the ground. We quickly dragged the guy out through the door with us. The door shut quietly behind us. Then we saw it wasn't a man at all. It was a woman, wings tattooed on her face, her jaw askew and mouth bleeding. She was still breathing, fortunately.

"Take her, Jones," I said. "Leave her here and they'll pursue us."

Jones nodded and threw the unconscious woman over his shoulder. We ran quickly across the grounds and reached the fence. Ward found the portion we'd cut and pushed it out. Behind us, I heard nothing. My visor showed no signs of pursuit. It seemed we had gotten away clean.

Half-way back to camp, a sudden sobbing groan from behind spun me around, rifle up. "It's the woman," Jones said. "She's waking up."

"She's a witness," Vero said. "They'll figure out it was a Wardogs operation."

"Plenty of people wear battlesuits," Zelag said.

The woman sobbed and moaned again.

"Don't be stupid," Vero said. "A team of people in the temple in the middle of the night, wearing battlesuits, not long after we were at the big event, wearing battlesuits. They'll have us ID'd before we could leave the planet. We can't have any witnesses."

"All right, you convinced me," Jones said, dropping the woman on the ground and drawing his Stark 3011.

"No!" exclaimed Vero. "What do you think you are doing? My God, you guys are insane. We just need to get her off the planet for a while."

"This is easier and faster," said Jones, racking a shot. "She won't feel nothing."

"No! No, you psychopath! We're in deep enough here without committing a murder," Vero spat. "Pick her up, that's an order! We'll ship her off-planet, fix her jaw, keep her quiet for a bit, then bring her back no worse for wear with some money in her account by way of apology. Zelag can put her out with his tranq."

The unlucky young woman blinked up at us from the ground, frightened and confused, then Zelag stuck her with the stunpen and she slumped back into unconsciousness.

"Women," Jones grumbled, putting away his Stark and picking up the injured cultist again. But despite his disgusted tone, he was surprisingly gentle with her. "You're a lucky little caterpillar, you are," he told her.

I checked my thermals as we neared the camp site. No one was around. No sign that anyone had been there while we were gone.

"I still think it would be safer to ice her," Ward muttered. "Even if they pay her off, she's a witness."

"To what," I said as we reached our camp. "Breaking and entering? We'll be long gone by the time they return her. And she didn't see nothing anyhow."

"Zip it, boys," Vero said as she removed her helmet and shook out her long hair. "The matter is settled. This is officially above your pay grade."

Chapter 6

"How can you stand watching grown men throw balls around with baskets on their arms?" Jones said as he sliced paper-thin strips off a sausage with a small vibroblade. He wore a blank facemask that obscured his features, as did Vero, Betti and I. Ward and Zelag were upstairs, probably playing games. Jones much preferred hands-on entertainment.

Green looked at him wide-eyed. He was zip-tied to a chair and sweating profusely.

"It just strikes me as being pretty boring," he continued, suddenly snipping off a third of the sausage and popping it in his mouth.

"Gambling," Green said, his voice cracking.

"What's that," Jones said, raising an eyebrow.

"The gambling, that's what makes it interesting."

"Yeah, now that makes sense." Jones nodded approvingly. "See, you get how this works. I ask the question and you answer it. No fuss, no blood, and nobody gets hurt."

"What do you want to know?" Green said, his voice cracking.

"DNA coding," said Vero.

This was our first interview, as Vero put it, with one of the three cultists we'd snatched. We had the others safely zipped and gagged in a closet. Not good times. Elsie was monitoring our victim's vital signs through a medical scanner Betti had set up. Betti told us the AI was so sensitive to physiological signals that she could tell if an interviewee was being truthful with almost perfect accuracy. Jones wasn't so sure, and insisted on a more traditional interrogation. We'd agreed to a compromise, combining traditional terror with intelligent tech, much to his delight.

"DNA?" said Green.

"We know your history," said Vero.

"And you need to talk to us if you'd like to have a future," said Jones, dropping the sausage and moving closer to Green. "You know, I always wanted to be a surgeon. But they said my hands weren't steady enough."

"Just tell me what you want to know!" Green said. "Please!"

"DNA coding," said Vero. "Did you engineer a designer toxin to assassinate Brixton Heiermach, the CEO of Datacon Verlag?"

"I didn't go to medical school either," Jones said ruefully, as he pointed the humming blade towards Green's stomach. "So I always wondered what a spleen looked like."

"Yes!" the man yelped. "Yes, dammit! Yes, I modified a toxin to target his DNA!"

"That was quick," Vero said.

"Maybe too quick?" Jones suggested, twirling the blade in a circle.

"No!" Green said. "No! It's the truth! I don't want to die!"

"He's telling the truth," Betti confirmed. Jones snorted.

"Tell us how you did it," Vero ordered.

"If you're familiar with how interrupting RNA polymerase II affects transcription rates, it's not that difficult. For example, the toxin Alpha-amantin can take transcription rates down to a half-dozen nucleotides per minute. Now imagine that instead we–"

"That's enough," said Vero. "We don't need to know all that. How was it delivered?"

"They put it in the ceremonial wine. In the chalice!"

"Not the champagne," I said.

"Your own chief druid drank from that chalice," said Vero. "And multiple other leaders. Yet you put it in the cup."

"It was perfectly safe!" Green said, his expression indicating that his professional pride was insulted. "It was very specifically coded. I know what I'm doing."

"Heiermach did nothing to you," Vero said.

"He insulted the holy mountain!" Green said. "Oh gods, I am a coward. I shouldn't be telling you this."

"Keep talking," Jones said, neatly removing a small piece of Green's collar. "Answer her questions."

"Who ordered you to code the DNA?" Vero asked.

Green gulped. "The… it was…"

"Tell us," Jones said, moving the blade upwards towards the man's left eye. "If you want to keep your sight."

"Bhagwan."

"Truth," Betti said.

"And was he the very top of the conspiracy?"

"Yes!" Green said.

"Lie," said Betti.

"I mean no!" Green said before Jones could make a move. "He was under the orders of Wandrell Perspix."

"Perspix is second in line for the position of chief druid," Betti said. "He's a very powerful member of the cult."

"Yes," said Green. "He ordered Bhagwan and Bhagwan ordered me to do it! Said I had to! For my soul!"

"So you obtained the toxin and coded it with your DNA magic," Vero said. "But who got you the stuff for you? That had to come from somewhere."

"That was also Bhagwan!" the man said. "He got the toxin for me! I was forced into it!"

"Anyone else?"

"No one else that I know of!"

Jones looked at Vero. "Can I cut him?"

"No!" Green said. "I swear by the mountain of the gods!"

"He's telling the truth," Betti said. "Elsie confirms it."

"Good enough for me," Vero said. "Put him out. We'll do Mr. Bhagwan next."

Bhagwan was tougher to crack. Jones had to cut him a little and smack him around before he was willing to talk.

"Stop!" he said, blood running down the side of his face. He spat a tooth on the floor. He was tough, I'll give him that.

"I directed the assassination!" he confessed. "I admit it!"

"Did you refine the toxin?" Vero asked.

"No," Bhagwan said. "I received the toxin after it was refined."

"At the temple?" Vero asked.

"No, we would never do it there! The temple is sacred!"

"Where then?"

Jones pressed at the nerve in the side of the man's neck and Bhagwan gasped in pain.

"A moon! A base!" Bhagwan hissed. "Dagona!"

"Dagona is a small moon owned by Takamoto Heavy Industries," Betti reported. "It circles the gas giant Tarmos in the Theemin system."

"Tell me who told you to do it," Vero said. "You didn't do this alone, did you?"

The man hesitated and Jones produced yet another knife. It was long and thin, and the lased-edge gleamed ominously silver. He touched the tip of the knife to Bhagwan's stomach, then ran it lightly down toward his crotch. "Want to hit the high notes, buddy?"

"No! Please, no! It wasn't me. It was Perspix! Perspix ordered the hit," Bhagwan gasped, trying to squirm away from the lethally sharp blade.

"He's lying," Betti said.

"Very good, Mr. Bhagwan," said Vero. "That wasn't so hard now, was it?"

Wintress looked around the room at us. His face was calm. "If you wish to kill me for my faith, I am ready to die."

"Oh you are, are you?" Jones said, displaying the yet-unused knife again.

"But we don't want you to die, Mr. Wintress," said Vero. "We only want you to tell us about the murder of Brixton Heiermach."

"I'm sorry?" Winters said. "Who is that?"

"The CEO of Datacon-Verlaag GmbH," Vero said. "The man your people murdered after the ceremony."

Winters shook his head. "Oh no, I know nothing about the murders. I would never do anything like that in any event! I'm no radical. You can ask anyone at the temple. I detest and abhor violence."

"So who did it?" Vero asked.

"If I knew, I would tell you," Winters said. "That is, assuming you represent a lawful operation and aren't merely seeking vengeance. Vengeance is for the gods, not men."

"Spare me the sermon, Mr. Wintress. I can assure you that we are government agents acting completely within the scope of the law," Vero lied without hesitation. "Now tell me, do you have any idea who might have been involved?"

"No," Wintress said. "None at all. I am afraid it may have been some of our more radical members who were responsible. The Chief Druid had accepted the corporation's repentance; he had promised peace and reconciliation. Many of us are quite upset that anyone would violate his promises.

"He's telling the truth," Betti reported.

"He is?" Jones said.

"Elsie says 99.995% chance."

"Very good," said Vero. "We apologize for any inconvenience, Mr. Winters."

"May I go?" he asked.

"Soon," she replied.

Vero and Betti disappeared and talked with Captain Williams, recorded a summary for whoever was running the op back on Kantillon, then came back to us with instructions for the next phase of our investigation. I wasn't privy to the conversation and wasn't exactly sure how the command structure was supposed to work between us and the investigators, but I knew my orders. They could do their detective stuff and we were to go along with whatever they decided and keep them safe. I had no need to tell them what to do and wasn't sure I could, but if it came to dangerous wetwork, I'd take the lead if necessary.

Zelag and I were tapped to take Green in to the local police. Jones and Vero had convinced the guy to sign a full confession. Now all we needed to do was drop him off.

Green rode quietly in the back of the Chrysota Plasmatix one of the team had acquired for us to use as a town car. The truck was gone, just in case it could be linked with our extracurricular activities at the temple. We wore our battlesuits despite the low chance of engagement. In our newly minted legal role as private investigators, we were allowed to be armed and the police had to leave us alone, but their agitation in our presence was obvious. We were polite and respectful this time, though, and the prisoner drop-off went off without a hitch. The processing officer even thanked us for doing our civic duty!

I wondered what WDI was going to do with Bhagwan. Despite his attempt to fob off the responsibility on Wintress, he was the guy who directed the operation. If he were turned over to the police, there was a very good chance that the charges would be dropped. We had no evidence, and the fact that we'd tortured him would not only get us in trouble, it might well help him evade justice. Well, it wasn't in my hands. We'd see what the brass wanted soon enough.

When we got back to the safe house my concerns about Bhagwan vanished as soon as I saw an unmarked black van in the driveway. A couple of local WDI contractors were wheeling out a man-sized shape in a black bodybag.

"Bhagwan," Zelag said, and I nodded in satisfaction. One less caterpillar.

Vero waved to us from the door as we approached.

"This your doing?" I asked, jerking a thumb at the meatwagon in the drive.

"He died of a overdose," Vero said, waving us inside. "Betti did the honors."

Betti smiled at us unapologetically as she poured a cup of coffee.

"Better than he deserved," Zelag said. "He went fast and painless. Not like poor Heiermach."

"Sorry," Betti said. "We're short on time."

"What did you do with Wintress?" I asked.

"Jones and Ward have taken him back to his family," Betti said. "He'll keep his mouth shut. Want some coffee?"

"Sure," I said. "One cream–"

"One sugar," Betti interrupted, smiling at me. You know, she was pretty cute. I smiled back at her, took the cup, and hoped I hadn't done anything that would inspire her to anything else in it.

"Drink up, Falkland," said Vero. "While you were out we got our orders."

"Yeah?" I said.

"Yeah. You want them now or you want to wait for Ward and Jones to return?"

"I'll wait for the guys," I said, sitting down in a recliner and leaning back in it. "I think I'm going to shut my eyes."

"Nappachino," said Zelag, nodding as he took a second chair.

"What?" I said.

"A nappachino. Chug some coffee, then take a quick nap. You wake up like a hurricane. Major power up."

I swigged my coffee and shut my eyes. Why not? I'll give it a try.

Two minutes later, the proximity chime rang and I opened my eyes.

"Jones and Ward are back," I heard Betti say. I jumped up and greeted the guys as they entered. So much for the nap experiment.

"Success?" I asked as they came in.

"Oh yeah, cute kids. Great time," Jones said. "Too bad the wife had tats on her face, though."

"I thought she was cute," Ward said.

Jones snorted. "I'll bet you also like it when chicks pierce their–"

"That's enough," I said, cutting Jones off. "We got orders."

Betti transferred the data packet to the tri-D. The message was short and simple.

Dispose of the identified party at your earliest convenience. Williams.

"Excellent," Ward said with satisfaction. "Looks like we are the tools of the gods."

Chapter 7

"He's a busy man," Betti said, continuing her overview of our target. It was seven in the morning and we sipped at our coffee while letting Silver Eyes do her thing. I'd gotten a good night's sleep despite Ward's snoring. He and I shared one room, Jones and Zelag shared another, and Betti and Vero were in the third. Now we were back to work, bright and early.

"Attends art exhibitions and charity dinners, meets with politicians. Vegetarian and promotes fitness. Quite ambitious. Despite his outwardly genial approach, he is very much a religious hardliner. He has links to terror cells off planet and was also the primary force behind the uprising against DVG. When he was younger he served a six-year prison sentence for the attempted assassination of an opposition party leader. Lives in New Patras Heights. Gated community."

"What's his digital security look like?" I asked.

"Very good," Betti said. "Better than the temple grounds."

"Can you crack his home AI?"

She shook her head, then brushed an errant strand of hair behind her ear. "Elsie already tried. His system has supernova-level firewalls. She was almost cracked when she tried what she thought was a gap and only recovered by jettisoning the affected chunk of her memory."

"How come a religious guru has that kind of AI?" Jones asked. "I mean, he's rich and powerful, but still. That's like, government-level, right?"

Betti nodded. "Money is no object for him. Another second and Elsie would have been compromised. She says she won't try again."

"So we do things the old-fashioned way," Vero said. "We watch him, figure out the patterns, then whack him."

"Vero," said Jones. "Has anyone ever told you you're a very, very att–"

"Shut up, Jones," Vero said, not unkindly.

"So we can't get into his house," I said. "Is there any way we can find out what he's likely to be doing. Maybe based on electronic correspondence?"

Betti nodded. "Elsie says she can monitor at least some of the incoming digital traffic, possibly giving us some of the messages he receives."

"So we can read his mail?" Ward said.

"Some of it," Betti said. "We may also be able to trace some of his activity by monitoring his secretary."

"The secretary isn't in his house?" Vero asked.

"No," said Betti. "He's located in one of the temple buildings. And we already know that's hackable."

"At the moment," Vero said.

"Does Perspix travel to work?" I asked.

"No, not often," Betti replied. "He has a security detail when he does. Six guys."

"Paranoid little caterpillar, ain't he?" Jones said.

"Elsie thinks she can get us more info when his secretary logs in at the temple this morning," Betti said. "Probably around eight hundred."

"Great," I said. "Let's get some breakfast while we wait."

New Patras Heights lay amidst slightly rolling hills on the remains of an ancient olive grove. It was one of those neighborhoods where you can leave your girl, your convertible and your wallet anywhere and know they won't be molested—unless they were somehow in violation of code. Once you went through the gate, the cobblestone roads wound in between elderly olive trees lit at night with softly changing accent lights. The streets were laid out in wobbling spokes with small crossroads completing blocks, the main roads extending from a circular central commons with a community center, theater, gym and swimming pools. In front of the community building was an ancient oil press, allegedly from Old Earth: a stone wheel standing in a stone base. I could see the slight shimmer of a protective field around it, shielding it from the elements and the local children, provided any of the latter even lived in the neighborhood. There was a distinct gentility to the place and I doubted hover races, kite drones or slingball would be smiled upon.

Today we were pretending to remodel a house two doors down from Wandrell Perspix's home. The neighborhood surveillance AI had decent security protocols but they were not nearly good enough to keep Elsie out. Thanks to the neighborhood sensor grid, any time Perspix left his house we knew it.

The house we were pretending to work on was owned by a banker for the revolutionary government of Morchard. Elsie had broken into his schedule and determined that he wasn't due back on the planet for a month. We dressed in work clothes and drove a beater Fiero van WDI had procured for us from the owner of an ailing handybot company. WDI had paid extra to keep the handybot—and to have the owner wait a few days on switching off the license on the van. The bot was a gangly thing that introduced itself as O'Reilly.

"Where do I start, sirs?" it asked as we walked into the expansive living room of our observation post.

"How about jumping in the pool?" Jones replied.

"Sir, if I were to do that, I would cease to function. If pool repair is required, drainage must first be effected, then I will gladly–"

"Shut up, bot," I said. "Jones isn't serious. We'd like you to work on–"

I looked around, trying to find something that wouldn't cause any serious changes to the house.

"Go ahead and work on cleaning the grout on the bricks around the fountain out front," I said. "And clean those gnomes, too."

The bot turned and dutifully wheeled its way to the car to retrieve its tools.

"If anything happens to that bot it's coming out of your paycheck, Jones," I said.

"Bot-lover," he said.

Ward was setting up a directional mic at the window facing Perspix's place. Chances are with all the other security our target would have a dampening field, but you never know. You got to try all angles. Along with the mic we placed a camera with face-tracking algo. It would shoot pics of anyone coming in or out, then send the images to Betti and Elsie. Simple stuff. And tedious to monitor. We just wanted to get a good idea of his movements and nail him at the right time. He was a moderately important man whose death would be investigated, so this hit had to look like an accident. It would be easy enough to send up a drone and have it nail him with a needle gun, but that was too likely to be picked up by a camera somewhere.

For the next two days we watched people come and go while inventing various jobs for O'Reilly. The homeowner was going to be delighted with how clean everything was upon his return. We even had the bot re-varnish the railings on the porch.

Perspix was in his fifties, but he kept himself in shape. As expected, we couldn't listen to him through the walls of his house but the mic let us hear him grunting every morning as he lifted weights on his back patio. He'd lift for about twenty minutes, then leave the house for a jog around the neighborhood. Then he'd come back, sometimes leaving during the day to meet with people in town. He entertained no visitors at the house itself.

His exercise habit gave us the opening for which we were looking. We'd identified a spot where there were two houses with tall privacy fences. The house on the other side of the road was obscured by a thick hedge, though there was a gap in the hedge where a utility box was located for repair access. Behind the box was a small piece of privacy fencing, blocking the view to the road. There were two cameras with views of that location but Elsie had turned them slightly to obscure Ward's location. When Perspix went around the corner, Ward would step out of that gap and nail him with a stunpen loaded with a heart-disrupting drug. The drug would take effect in two or three seconds. Perspix would clutch his chest and fall to the ground, the apparent victim of a heart attack. We'd drive by in our Fiero the next block over and pick Ward up as he walked calmly down the street. The whole affair would be done and dusted in less than thirty seconds.

Ward had insisted on pulling the trigger. He wanted to balance the scale on behalf of Heiermach. "I owe it to his family," he'd told me.

I told him it wasn't his responsibility but he remained unconvinced, so I told him to go for it. Why not. One of us had to do it.

Now we were just a few hectasecs from go. O'Reilly was scrubbing at the already gleaming tile in the bathroom while we listened to the mic and watched Perspix's house on a flatfoil display we'd linked to the camera. It was a nice piece of tech and new for us. You could crumple it in a ball and shove it in your pocket like a piece of foil, then spread it out flat and stick it to a surface. It had a slight static charge that kept it adhered to almost anything and it could be keyed to display any feed you liked. It had taken a matter of seconds to link it to our camera and it was safer to watch the screen in another room than for us all to stand in the window and stare across the road. Ward had left the house two kilosecs previously and we were listening to Perspix lift weights.

"That's his third set," Jones said. "Now he stretches, then comes the run."

Perspix walked around the tasteful flagstone walk beside his house and leaned against the cedar in his front yard to start his stretches.

One leg, then the other. Now the shoulder roll. Now touching the toes…

"He's off!" Zelag announced.

"Dog Two, he's on his way," I said through the con. "You have the green light."

"Roger that, Dog One," acknowledged Ward, sounding eager.

"All right, let's pack up and roll, men," I said, then called the bot. "O'Reilly, load up."

"But sir, I have not completed the task to which I have been set," the bot replied. "If I may just continue for another 248 seconds, I'll have it properly cleaned."

"Get in the van, buddy," I said. "Don't give Jones an excuse to shut you down."

The machine made a sad bloop and rolled past us without another word. I glanced around to make sure we hadn't missed anything. We had the camera, the screen, the mic... okay, time to go. I casually strolled to the van, climbed in, and fired it up. The other two were inside, as was the bot. Elsie would lock the house behind us, then the house AI would wake up with a mild case of amnesia.

"Dog One, we have a problem," Ward said softly over the intercom.

"You get him?" I said.

"Negative," he replied. "There's someone else with him."

"What?" I said. "A neighbor?"

"Negative," Ward said again. "I captured his face and sent it to Dog Watch already. We haven't seen this guy before. Looks like it might be a planned meeting."

"On a jog?" I said, but Ward remained silent.

I cursed, then drove the van around the block to our pick-up location.

"Dog One," Ward whispered again. "I can take them both out. They're walking towards me now."

"Negative on that, Dog Two," Betti's voice broke in. "I'm not finding anything on this guy. Something is off here."

"Great," I muttered, then keyed the com. "Abort, Dog One. Repeat: abort! Do not engage!"

"Copy that. Oh, hey. Good morning," I heard Ward say. Then there was something unintelligible, but it sounded like a simple exchange of greetings. Then I heard Ward again. "No, nothing serious. Just scheduled maintenance."

Seconds ticked by, then minutes. A woman was half-dragged past our Fiero by four big grey dogs on leashes. I waved and she almost let go to wave back, then thought better of it and nodded at me instead. I watched her disappear around a row of rose bushes.

"Dog One?" came a voice at long last.

"Here," I replied.

"Coming to your position," Ward said.

A minute later he jumped in the van.

"He saw me," Ward said. "And the other guy. Thin guy. Oriental. They knew each other. It was almost certainly an arranged meeting."

"Was he suspicious?" I asked.

"Couldn't tell for sure, but I think so," said Ward. "We may need another plan."

"Yeah," I said. "Not your fault. Just bad luck." I gunned the van out of the neighborhood and back towards our safe house. Maybe Vero would have a better idea.

"We're getting data on Perspix's friend," Vero said. "It took Betti a lot longer than usual. This guy has multiple profiles. Name seems to be James Hozumi. He's almost certainly a corporate spook for Takamoto Heavy Industries."

"Wait," I said. "Aren't they the ones with the moon?"

"One and the same," Vero said. "I've forwarded what we've found to SHQ."

"I should have nailed them both," Ward said, sitting on a recliner. "I knew it!"

"No, you did exactly the right thing," Vero said. "Always abort when the plan goes haywire. The book is clear on that. Don't worry, we'll make a proper hitter out of you yet."

"Definitely," said Betti. "Actually, this is starting to look like it's more valuable than a clean kill. You did good."

"Thanks," Ward said. "Now we'll have to come up with another plan for taking him out, though."

Jones walked in, Red Newt in hand. "Anyone else want a beer?"

"No," I said. "I could use some coffee though."

I looked out the window at our Fiero. O'Reilly had gotten out on his own and was sweeping the driveway.

"How can you not like that bot?" I asked Jones.

"Jones doesn't like being reminded what a slob he is," Ward said.

"Too bad we have to get rid of him," Zelag said, using his metal fingers to pop a beer of his own. "I'll bet we could train him to clean our guns."

"I like to clean my own guns," Jones said. "And I'll have you know–"

"Falkland," Betti interrupted from the next room. "New orders."

I walked in to read the message already posted to the tri-D.

Disposal canceled. Capture both targets of interest, then await further orders. Williams.

"Great," said Ward. "Another kidnapping. I knew I should have just killed him."

"Maybe you'll still get your chance," Vero said. "It's happened before."

"I agree," I said. "The captain or his higher-ups are chasing this string. Maybe we'll unwind something big. Wouldn't it be more satisfying to take down a bunch of guys on behalf of dear departed Heiermach?"

The suggestion met with a general rumble of agreement.

"We need to figure out a good place to nab the two of them," Zelag said.

"Catching them together won't be easy," Jones said. "Could be months until their next meeting."

"Agreed," I said. "We'll have to take them separately. Bettina, can you track Hozumi?"

"Working on it," she said.

"Good," I said. "Now, about Perspix. I'm not keen on hanging out in his neighborhood anymore. That feels like pushing our luck."

"It's not the only option," Vero said. "Betti has now hacked his daily schedule, thanks to his secretary."

"Carter Pettibone," Betti said.

"I thought the house AI was capable of catching Elsie?"

"It is," Bettina chimed in. "But Pettibone and Perspix have a shared calendar file. I can read it live, even when Perspix makes changes and additions from his house."

"Awesome," I said.

"She really should've met Four-Eyes," Ward said. "They could have raised a happy little family of AIs together."

"Four-eyes?" Vero asked.

"Old friend," I replied. "Hey Betti, you see anything on the schedule that looks likely?"

Betti paused, then spoke. "He's got a meeting with a real estate developer tomorrow. Restaurant."

"Too public," Vero said.

"Depends on the restaurant," Jones said. "One of those dark ones with booths could be good. Especially if it's got a VIP entrance."

"Day after tomorrow he's supposed to tour a park before it opens," Betti said.

"That sounds promising," Vero said.

"Maybe," I said. "What kind of park?"

Betti's eyes flicked around for a moment. "Land was owned by a wealthy widow. She became a Chrysalan a decade ago. Decided to make this a postmortem donation. It will contain an education center, a walk-through holographic recreation of the temple, picnic areas, an outdoor speaking circle, etc. It's sandwiched between an agricultural school and the Sparta zoo."

"Lots of bushes?" Ward asked.

Betti nodded. "There's a botanical garden in progress. It may not be completely filled out yet."

"I like the restaurant," Jones said. "What type of place is it?"

"The Luscious Leek," Betti said. "Describes itself as 'Sino-Fusion with a vegetarian focus.' They group people around grills where you cook your courses as they arrive."

"Roasted green things," Zelag snorted.

"Just knowing these places exist makes me want to kill everyone in it," Jones said. "Forget the park. Let's nuke the restaurant!"

"Hell no!" Vero protested. "You cannot be serious!"

"He isn't," I said.

"Sure I am," Jones protested, wounded.

"I think the park is our best option," Ward broke in.

"Agreed," I said. "Park makes more sense anyhow. Cover, more routes to exfil, what's not to like?"

"He'll have bodyguards," Betti said. "Looks like two of them. His regulars."

"No problem," I said. "They're not Wardogs. So what's the occasion?"

"All I know from the calendar is he's going to be meeting with Mrs. Larsfeld—that's the widow—and getting a tour."

"I thought she was dead?" Jones looked puzzled.

"She's not dead yet," Zelag snorted. "She's giving them the land in her will."

"Oh."

"Sounds custom-made for us," Vero said. "I want in this time."

"Why?" I asked. "We can handle this."

She looked at me with a withering glare. "In a public operation, a female agent is almost always an asset."

"So you read the book," I said, secretly impressed. "All right. Me, you and Zelag will take this guy."

"What about us?" Ward said indignantly.

"You had your shot," I said. "You, Jones and Betti will track the corporate spook. We need eyes on him—he can't leave the planet. Which reminds me, you know where he is now, Betti?" She nodded. "Good," I said. "You three work out a plan on taking him and let me know what you come up with. I'd like to get a good look at this park first. Vero, Zelag, you two up for some recon?"

"Sure," said Vero. "But I also need to do some shopping."

"What?" I said.

"We'll need to fit in better at the park."

"It's not open to the public yet. Won't we be conspicuous already?"

"Not really," Betti chimed in. "People have been using it for romantic assignations, nature walks and fishing for a long time."

"Great," I said, and turned back to Vero. "Jack in and shop in the car."

"Sounds like a plan," Vero said. "But please tell me we're not taking the van or the robot."

I looked out the front window where O'Reilly was now carefully edging the driveway. He looked up and waved.

"Fine," I sighed, feigning disappointment. "We'll take the Chrysota."

Driving out to the park with Vero at my side was probably the most normal thing I'd done in a long time. I watched the GPS while she shopped on the net. I snuck a glance at her and thought about being married—honest-to-goodness shackled—to a woman. Not necessarily her. Just a good-looking woman who could sit two feet away and ignore me.

Nope, not for you, Tommy. I made too much money with Wardogs and lived a life of high risk. Even a long-term relationship with a woman seemed like a bad idea. Not much benefit in it anyhow, other than raising up some little Wardogs of my own.

We reached the park and checked it out. Not much to see, but there were multiple locations we could hide, plus it didn't seem too busy.

Vero and I noted various locations which might work for an ambush, then got back in the car and headed to the safe house.

One the return trip I thought about asking her about family and her past and all that, then decided not to bother. It was easier to just shut up and drive.

When we got back Ward and Jones were both out but Betti was in her normal spot at the table, lost in the net. Vero disappeared into her room and I grabbed a Newt from the fridge—and then almost dropped it as I heard a buzzing sound outside the house. Then the proximity alarm went off. Zelag grabbed for his gun but I already had my Reaper in hand. I waved them down and approached the door—something was just outside.

"It's your delivery," Betti said from behind me. I looked out the wavy transparent aluminum window and saw a drone drop a package and take off again.

"Geez," I said, jamming the Reaper back in its holster. I opened the door and picked up the box, then tossed it on the table.

"Oh good!" Vero said, emerging from her room. She'd changed into jeans and a white T-shirt. "They're here!"

She ripped into the box and pulled out various soft, smaller packages. "Here," she said to Zelag, pushing some packages his way. "This is for you. And this. And this." She pushed a few more to me. "Here, Tommy. These are for you."

I ripped open my packages. A red pair of shorts, a ballcap and a T-shirt. I read the front of it and shook my head. "You have to be kidding me."

"What?" said Vero, acting innocent.

Zelag took it from my hands, held it up, then read it. "Earth. Sky. Love." He snickered and tossed it back to me.

"I'd like to see what she got you," I said to Zelag. He looked down at his unopened packages with a stricken look on his face. Vero blinked innocently at us both.

Zelag extended a short blade from one of his metal fingers and sliced through the packaging, then took out a pair of khaki slacks, a fanny pack and a shirt of his own. A collared one with what appeared to be shell buttons. Instead of a message, it featured an intertwining pattern of fish, birds and flowers in the brightest, most hideous colors imaginable.

"Holy space, Vero," Zelag said as he stared at the shirt. "Remind me to never, ever ask you for advice on what to wear."

I looked down at the last package on the table. "What's that?"

"This one's mine," she said, ripping it open and holding up the contents. It was a little pink-and-green sundress.

"You're going on an op in that?" I asked. There wasn't much to it.

"There are more ways to take out a target than brute force," she said coyly.

"Glad I don't have to wear that," Betti chimed in. "I wouldn't want anyone seeing the you-know-what on my you-know-where."

"Your what?" Zelag said.

"Never mind," said Vero. "She's sensitive about it."

"Great," I said, picking up my pile. "I'm going to look like a complete retard in this outfit."

"That's the idea, Falkland," Vero said, smiling sweetly.

Chapter 8

It was a sunny morning with a slight breeze. Vero had prepared a picnic basket and spread a blanket in a field just outside the main section of the park. She'd also brought a slingball, which Zelag and I threw back and forth. We looked like three fruitcake friends spending the day off work to get stoned in the park. Zelag was way too good at throwing with his stupid metal arm. He'd zip the sling and whack the ball into my chest so hard I felt like I was getting bruises, and he never missed. This unnatural accuracy was part of our plan, but for now, it was annoying. A guy and his kid were down by the water behind us playing with a little aquatic drone. Occasionally people wandered by and waved or nodded to us. No one gave us a second look. Well, not me or Zelag, anyhow.

As we played, Betti fed us tracking data on our target.

"He's getting out of his car," she said. "Mrs. Larsfeld and the park manager are in the reception center. He's heading toward them. Two guards, as expected, fore and aft."

I looked at Vero. "You ready?"

She smiled and batted her eyelashes. I rolled my eyes. "Don't overplay it now."

There was a spot along the path where a sweeping bougainvillea hedge had been planted. The path itself led up towards the holographic temple recreation. The park was engineered to move people towards that central focus and we were 99 percent certain that our target would pass by our location. The widow and the park director were a little bit of trouble, but Betti had a plan for them as well.

If Vero could distract the bodyguards, we'd hit them with the stunners first, then neutralize our target. I was starting to regret not bringing Jones or Ward, though I knew the two of them were now busy monitoring our second target from the roof of an apartment building.

Focus, Tommy. Stay in the moment. I felt the adrenaline rising as I spotted Perspix for the first time. He was walking out of the reception area with Mrs. Larsfeld and the manager. Behind them were two beefy guys in shades. Both guards had tattooed heads and more muscle than human bodies normally produce without injected hormones. I was pretty sure Zelag and I could take them hand-to-hand, but we might have to seriously hurt them to incapacitate them. They moved like they were trained, and their positioning was professional, close to their client without being right on top of him.

They walked closer to our position. Zelag and I threw the ball back and forth as they approached.

I saw Mrs. Larsfeld put her hand to her ear, then speak to someone. A call. Gotta be Bettina. Come on… go, go, go, I thought to myself. Larsfeld touched Perspix's sleeve and said something to the park manager, then held up a finger to Perspix with what looked like an embarrassed apology. Back in a minute, I thought. Then she and the manager walked back towards the reception area, leaving Perspix alone with his guards. Whatever Betti had used to distract her, it had worked.

"Go," Vero whispered over the com.

Zelag threw the ball in a long arc into the row of bougainvilleas about 10 meters behind the guards.

"I'll get it!" Vero yelled in a sing-song voice, then skipped her way over to the hedge. She dashed right into the thorny mess, then squealed, her short sundress caught in the thorns. "Oh no!" she said. "Oh dear! Help! I'm stuck!"

I saw Perspix eye her up and down, then smile and nod at his guards. They moved towards her and Zelag and I followed suit. Meanwhile, Vero struggled helplessly, letting her dress ride up her hip and making pained little squeals. I'm sure some of them were real, actually. Those hedges were nasty. She already had a few bleeding scratches on her arms, chest and legs. I had to give it to her. The woman was all in.

"Hey, quit thrashing about," one of the guards told her. "Just hold still, we'll get you out."

"Oh, thank you!" she said.

"These things will grab you," said the other guard, working Vero's hair out of a branch.

"Well, golly, Shelly!" I said, prancing up to the hedge. "You really got yourself stuck good!"

The guards looked me over with about the same expression you'd give a retarded puppy, then went back to freeing Vero.

Meanwhile, Zelag slipped around the fence and jabbed a stunpen into his guard, taking him down. I did the same to mine, but he collapsed on top of me and his weight took me down. It wasn't my fault, he was just that big.

"Tommy!" Vero shrieked, somehow producing her Bobcat from I have no idea where. I pushed the dead weight off me just in time to see Perspix coming at me brandishing a vibroblade! I struggled to find my stunpen, but somehow, I had dropped it. Zelag raised his sidearm but Vero was faster. POW! She hit Perspix right in the chest with her first shot, then followed it with a second, a third, and at least three more shots!

He went down to the ground hard, his skin red with burns, the knife humming harmlessly by his side.

Dammit.

Zelag went to check his pulse, but I already knew it wouldn't be there. He wasn't breathing.

"Holy shit," Zelag whispered. "He's dead!"

Vero's arms were trembling and she still held the gun pointed at Perspix's crumpled body. "But I used stun!" she said. She looked at the setting on her Bobcat and held it up to show us. "Look! I just stunned him!"

"He's dead," I said. "Put your gun away."

She did, slowly and shakily tucking it into the holster on her upper thigh. "But I had it set to stun," she repeated.

Zelag put his hand up to his forehead and shook his head. "What do we do now, Tommy?"

"Maybe he had a bad heart." Vero suggested hopefully.

"Pull yourself together, Parey," I told her. "First thing is we need to get him out of here. We don't want the park manager and the widow to find us with a body."

Vero was still shaking. "All I did was stun him! I didn't try to kill him."

Zelag shook his head as he grabbed our target's feet and dragged him right through the hedge. We'd decided to leave the guards alive, so it would look like a kidnapping, not a hit.

We quickly got Perspix's body down the hill to our picnic area where Zelag pulled two grav lifts out of the basket and zip-tied them to the body so it would drift it above the ground instead of dragging it all over. Doing all this without a battlesuit was really a pain in the ass, I decided.

I saw the kid at the river look up at us and I waved to him as we floated the body into the small pomegranate orchard at the back of the park. He waved cheerfully back with a smile. His dad didn't even look up. We'd parked our vehicle on a small farm road that ran behind the park alongside the zoo. The orchard was a good place to get quickly out of sight for now.

"Goddammit," Vero muttered. "I thought I could handle it."

"It happens," Zelag said.

"I don't know what happened," she said. "He wasn't supposed to die!"

"You hit him five or six times," I said. "One stun is tough enough on the nervous system. Three or four shots in quick succession will overwhelm it."

"Damn, damn, damn," she cursed. "I'm supposed to be in charge here! I'm going to get in serious trouble with corporate! I should have just stayed on overwatch."

"Hey, relax," Zegal said. "It's not like you killed someone decent."

"I don't care about that creep," she snapped. "I care about my career! This makes me look like an inept hothead. I blew the whole damn op! I've run plenty of ops before. Once I even infiltrated a revolutionary government! I had one simple thing to do here—bring in a cultist— and I blew it!"

She was shaking and balling and unballing her fists, unable to control herself.

"Listen Vero, calm down," I said. "Just shut up, will you? We'll cover for you."

"How!?" she said. "How can you cover for this!?" She slapped Perspix's body. "I killed our damn mark!"

"Wardogs watch each other's backs," I said, then sniffed the air. "What is that awful smell?"

"Animals," Zelag said. "What they leave behind, to be more specific."

"Oh yeah. The zoo isn't far from here." And then I had a brilliant idea. An idea so inspired and wonderful it almost made me laugh.

"Look, we'll figure out our story later," I said, grabbing her by the shoulder. "First we need to do a little clean up." I keyed my com. "Betti—we need to get into the zoo."

"The zoo?" she said. "The one you're close to now? I have you in the little orchard to the west of it."

"Yeah, exactly. I need you to tell me which animals will devour a body the fastest. I mean everything, bones and all, not just the meat." Vero's mouth dropped open and I winked at her. Zelag grinned and I nodded at him. "Listen in, Zelag."

There was silence for a moment. Then Betti spoke. "The ferrosaurs are your best bet."

"Where are they?" I asked.

"Go around the back of the zoo until you come to a concrete wall. On the other side of that is the ferrosaur pen. Be careful, though. They're a three-meter tall meat-eating raptor and they're aggressive."

"How can we get into the pen? The fence has gotta be tall, right?"

She was quiet for a few moments, then replied. "Yes, it's a high one. 10 meters or so. But there's a lighting pole built into the wall. You might be able to climb it, then throw the body over."

"No problem," Zelag said. He was right. With the anti-grav ties, we could float it op and toss it in.

"We can do it," I said, then I heard a far-off scream. "Uh oh. Sounds like widow what's-her-name just found the guards. Betti, get those cameras and sensors off. We're going for it."

"You got it," she said.

Vero followed us quietly to the back of the zoo, still looking shaky. All her bravado had disappeared. Screwing up and killing someone can be hard, especially if it's the first time.

It took a few minutes to reach the zoo but we moved as fast as we could. The smell of manure got stronger, along with a rank reptilian odor like burned cheese and old piss.

"There's the pole," Zelag said, dialing up the juice on the grav lifts until Perspix's body floated like a macabre balloon. Though the pole was smooth and metallic, he was able to grip it firmly with his cybernetic arm. It was probably magnetized, I concluded. I was starting to understand why he hadn't opted for a flesh-and-blood replacement. He pulled himself quickly up the pole. Once at the top, he dialed down the grav lifts until the dead man stopped rising, removed the ties, then shoved the unlucky corpse down into the enclosure.

From the other side of the wall came a gurgling hiss, then excited shrieks that sounded like tearing metal, followed by the sound of enthusiastic snapping and crunching.

"Dear God," Vero said, making a face.

"Wow, they're really getting into it," Zelag said cheerily, looking down into the pen. "Good thinking, Tommy! That's it! Get the head too!"

"Jack, get down," I said. "We gotta vacate the premises so she can turn the lights back on."

We raced back to the Chrysota and took off for home base. I set the car on auto, then looked over at Vero in the passenger seat. Her dress was ripped and torn, and she had scratches all over her legs and arms, just starting to scab up. Her eyes were rimmed with red and she stared straight ahead, gnawing at her lower lip.

"Listen, Vero," I said.

She looked at me.

"It happens. No plan ever survives contact with the enemy. Now stop beating yourself up. I told you we'd cover for you."

"How?" she said.

"We'll tell them I shot him. Just trust me, will you? It's gonna be okay."

She stared at me in silence for a long moment, then nodded.

"Good girl."

Chapter 9

On the way home we got word from Jones that their team had picked up Hozumi in a parking lot as he was exiting his personal vehicle. Their enthusiasm came through the com, deepening Vero's frustration at our failure.

When we got back to the safe house, I got my first look at Mr. Hozumi. Jones had tied him to a cot in the basement and he was still out.

"Betti took him," Jones said. "Nice and slick. He never even saw her coming. She's not half bad in the field when she's not staring off into the distance communing with the AI gods."

"Excellent," I said. "Well done!"

Hozumi was a thin, older man with gray hair and lines around his eyes. His haircut looked expensive.

"Betti says Elsie picked up some implants in the guy," Ward said. "Nothing scary, though. Optics, some organ enhancements, an augment in his brain."

"I wonder what being a corporate spook pays," Jones said.

"Why do you care, Jonesie? You have to be smart to get jobs like that," Ward said.

"Speaking of smart, I need to call Captain Williams and give him the sitrep," I said.

"Yeah, what happened out there?" Jones said. "I heard you killed your guy?"

"Yeah, I had no choice," I lied. "I got tangled up with one of the guards on the ground, Perspix pulled a blade and was going for Parey, so I had to take him out before he gutted her. Only had time for a headshot, and that was all she wrote."

"Damn," Ward said. "I wanted to kill him."

"Is Parey all right?" Jones said, his brow furrowed.

"She's cool," I said, hoping Vero had the good sense to keep her pretty mouth shut. "We dumped the body in the pen of some very hungry lizards. They'll never find him."

"Good idea," Jones said. "HQ is gonna be pissed, though. They wanted to interrogate him."

"They'd have been a lot more pissed if he'd let the guy kill Parey," Ward pointed out. "Protecting her and Silver Eyes is our top priority."

"Yeah, exactly," I agreed. Ward was right. HQ wasn't going to bite my head off for following my orders.

I went to my room and locked the door before making my call. I didn't need any distractions. I ran through the events of the day, settled the story in my head, then keyed in Williams's office on the little tri-D on the dresser.

I got a secretary, who sent me to an aide, who eventually put me through to the captain. He was leaning down over his desk and looking into the screen, a jacket slung over one shoulder.

"Evening, Falkland. You caught me on the way out. Did you secure the targets?"

"One of them," I replied.

"One? Perspix? Already saw he's reported missing."

"No sir," I replied. "We got Hozumi. Perspix is KIA."

He frowned and sat down at his desk. "Who screwed up?"

"No one," I said. "Zelag and I were dealing with his guards and the target pulled a vibroblade. Veronique had been the decoy and she was in imminent danger, so I followed my orders."

"Your orders were to take him alive."

"My primary orders are to keep her alive, sir. My call, sir. I stand by it."

He pulled out a pipe and packed it, then lit it and took a few puffs. I don't know if he was trying to make me sweat or not, but I simply waited him out. "All right, Falkland. In my opinion, you made the right call."

"Thank you, sir," I said, careful not to let any relief show on my face.

"Well, it can't be helped now," Captain Williams said with a shrug. "Hozumi is the more important target anyhow. Veronique and Bettina giving him the workover yet?"

"Not yet, sir."

"Let me know what the girls find out," he said, tapping out his pipe into a disposal chute. "Don't accidentally kill him too, please."

The transmission ended. I let out a deep breath. I knew Zelag would be cool. As long as Vero's nerves held up and she kept her mouth shut, no one would ever know our little secret. As I expected, the brass weren't inclined to come down hard on one of their asskickers kicking a little too much ass. Hell, that was our motto, after all.

"I'm quite happy to talk," Hozumi said before Jones even started his usual intimidation routine. This time he'd brought in a banana and a razor blade. I think he lay in bed thinking up stuff like that.

"Ask me whatever you like," Hozumi continued. "I will tell you the truth. I have nothing to hide."

"He's telling the truth," Betti said. Jones looked disappointed.

"Good," Vero said. "We have plenty of questions for you."

"That's fine," Hozumi said. "I do have one condition, however."

Jones grinned and abruptly stood up from the chair he had been sulking on.

"What is is?" Vero said.

"Let me talk with my superiors at THI."

Jones frowned and sat back down. Vero pulled Betti aside for a short whispered conversation, then nodded and turned back to Hozumi. "You may speak to them. But be aware that we're recording. So, no funny business."

"May I have my transmitter?" Hozumi asked.

"Let me see it first," I said. Vero pulled the small earring-sized device from a plastic baggie she'd stowed in the closet and handed it to me. I looked at it, then turned to Betti. "Did you have Elsie check this thing out?"

She nodded. "It's a normal issue. Sonautic *Nebula*. You can buy them anywhere."

"Here you go," I gave it to Vero. She looked at me meaningfully, and visibly relaxed when I gave her a little nod. "I don't see anything wrong with it."

"Would you put it in my ear? Hozumi asked. "Unless you're willing to unzip my hands, that is."

Vero put it in his ear. Hozumi said something in Japanese, then started talking rapidly in some sort of coded language.

"Sounds like funny business," Jones said. "Want me to stop him?"

"What is he saying?" Vero said to Betti.

"Not sure," Betti said. "He's speaking in an encrypted language. Even Elsie has no idea what he's saying."

"Thank you," Hozumi said a moment later. "I apologize for not letting you listen in. It was considerably faster to speak that way."

"Fine," Vero said. "Now it's time for you to talk to us."

"Of course," Hozumi said. "Ask away."

"Let's start with the basics," Vero said. "Your name is James Hozumi, correct?"

"Yes. I am a development executive with Takamoto Heavy Industries."

Vero glanced at Betti. Betti nodded back at her.

"Good," Vero said. "Keep telling us the truth. Now, Mr. Hozumi, what did you have to do with the assassination of Brixton Heiermach?"

"I had nothing to do with it. But I am in the same business as you. I was investigating a problem I may have inadvertently caused."

"Investigating what kind of a problem?"

"A bioware technology leak."

"Go on," Vero said.

"I'll try to make it brief. Takamoto Heavy Industries was working with a small biotech company in the development of new technologies. One, for example, which would allow passenger liners to tailor their cabin experience directly to the physiology of consumers. It was one of many thousands of R&D projects we fund. Yet in the course of working with this particular company, one of our internal auditors felt something was "off" and launched a clandestine investigation into their operations."

"This is not precisely the truth, Mr. Hozumi," Betti said.

Hozumi swallowed and nodded. "I knew a bit more but failed to report it to my superiors as there was substantial profit involved in being quiet."

"Truth," Betti said.

"To my shame," he said. "As it happens, THI discovered their new partner also had their fingers deep into something unrelated to travel."

"What was that?" said Vero.

"The bioweapons."

"Which brings us around to the death of Mr. Heiermach," Vero said.

"Yes. This firm is developing very sophisticated bioweaponry, customized to targets. Much more lucrative than passenger comfort. When Takamoto found out, they discontinued their relationship and I have been put on probation. Obviously, my superiors would prefer to stay comfortably inside the legal lines drawn by the Terran Ascendancy, as if word about this illegal bioweapons research got out, it would seriously impede our ability to win government and military contracts."

"And harm your bottom line," Vero said. "We understand that. You must know, however, that I am working for WDI and we have our own priorities. When one of our clients is murdered in a very public way while supposedly under our protection, we feel we have a responsibility to ID and track down the perpetrators."

"Yes," Hozumi nodded. "We're in the same ship here. We would like to do the same, as we believe there is still a bit too much linking Takamoto to these despicable criminals."

"You said they terminated the contract," Vero said.

"Yes, but there was some issue on the timing, regretfully. The break wasn't exactly clean due to my indiscretion, therefore the company continued working with them for a period of time after they should have known about the problem. This might cause issues with our shareholders were that to go public, not to mention potential conflicts with the Terran Ascendancy…"

"No shit," Jones said.

"…and therefore, THI has now requested I request certain assistance from your fine company," Hozumi concluded.

Vero looked at Betti, who gave her a thumbs up.

"Your girl over there has an augment, I assume," Hozumi said.

"Yes," Vero said.

"Very good. Then you know I'm telling you the truth."

"Yes," said Vero. "But I'm not seeing how a small brush with a minor biotech company would be all that bad for Takamoto. If they kill a few people and you've now ended your relationship, so what? It was an oversight. They could just throw you under the bus and claim they had no knowledge. They're in the clear. THI can go its own way."

"It's worse than that," Hozumi said. "By the way, my wrists rather hurt. Would you mind?"

Vero nodded at Jones, who had peeled the banana and just taken a bite. He set the fruit on an end table, stood, and unzipped Hozumi's wrists.

"Thank you," Hozumi said.

"You said it was 'worse than that,' " Vero said. "Explain."

"Yes," said Hozumi. "You see, the biotech company isn't interested in little two-bit assassinations like the ones the Chrysalans pulled off. Heiermach was just a convenient test case for them. They used Bhagwan and Perspix as a beta test for a DNA-targeted plague."

"It was a salamander toxin," Betti broke in. "Not a plague."

"Of course it was," Hozumi said. "But you missed the delivery system."

"The chalice?" Vero said.

Hozumi shook his head. "It's a virus. Targeted to specific DNA. It replicates at an incredible rate, then releases a coded toxin, killing the host."

"What a minute," I said. "I saw a flick once where people caught a plague like that. One of the scientists in it said that fast-acting viruses killed people too quickly to spread properly. Isn't that true?"

"Yes," Hozumi said. "I'm no epidemiologist, but if I understand it correctly, a longer incubation period means people move a lot farther and can share a disease with a lot more folks before they succumb. But don't you think they know that as well? They're working on a plague here. A plague that can be used to wipe out segments of the population based on their genetic code. They could wipe out all..." he gestured at Vero. "...blondes, for instance. It would be a terrible thing if it got used. It's a horrible death, too. Cruel on purpose."

"How do you know all this, Mr. Hozumi?" Vero said.

"I was... now sharing all I knew with my superiors. We were close to finishing our contract and I worked on commission. Very lucrative. But THI has not been in business for this long without developing a sophisticated intel network," Hozumi said. "They started digging."

"What about your meeting with Perspix?" Vero said.

"I was attempting some damage control to see if I could get back into THI's good graces. Now it seems they have decided to control the damages without my assistance. Are you interested in a contract? It would be profitable for you, but most of all, it could very well save the galaxy."

Jones laughed. "I've been saving the galaxy since you were in diapers." Vero frowned at him. Jones was obviously much younger than Hozumi.

"Fine," I said, stepping in. "What is the mission?"

"There is a space station in the Gunwal system disguised as an asteroid. It's the facility where the plague is being created. If the virus is ever released and THI is linked even slightly to its development—even in the most oblique way—it will be hell to pay. We may not survive as a company. Therefore, they are offering WDI 10 million TA credits to deal with it."

Jones whistled.

"Deal with it?" Vero said. "How?"

"You are to wipe out all personnel on the station and destroy the laboratories. This business needs to end but we can't bring in the authorities. Too many questions."

"Can we do that?" Betti said.

"They are criminals," Hozumi replied. "Outside of the law."

"I can't say whether or not the brass will take your offer, Hozumi," Vero said.

"Wait a minute," Jones said. "The other guy said there was a moon in some other system, not an asteroid."

"He was deliberately misled, I am sure," Hozumi said. "We are in a better position to know, I assure you. Now, will you consider my offer?"

"I will contact the main office," Vero replied.

"Thank you," Hozumi said. "This is a very sensitive matter, however. I wish your assurance that you will only speak directly to your superior and that you will not involve any more mercenaries than are already here."

"Just the six of us?" Vero said. "You want us to take a base with six people?"

"It's probably a chintzy civilian operation," Jones said. "It's not that big a deal."

"Correct," said Hozumi. "Their defense is based on camouflage. They're in the middle of nowhere on an asteroid. They won't expect visitors. And I said six mercenaries. THI will provide at least one scientific professional as an investigator on their behalf, plus whatever other support personnel are required. I have been ordered to give you a 12-hour window in which to accept or reject this contract. If that time expires, we will seek other options."

"This whole thing stinks," Jones said. "I'm not quite trusting this guy, no matter what Elsie says. No offense, Betti."

Betti shrugged. "Unless he's a complete psychopath, Elsie can tell if he's telling the truth."

"What?" I said. "Pyschopaths can hide from an AI?"

Betti nodded. "Oh yes, but that's very rare. Still, some are able to disguise their emotional responses so completely that–"

"Shh," Vero said. "Not now. Alright, Jim. Let's just say we have some doubts about your story."

Hozumi nodded. "I understand and so do my superiors. After all, you caught me in contact with a known assassin. You will get in touch with Mr. Akio here on Feymanus and let him know whether you accept or decline this arrangement. As a token of Takamoto's sincerity, they are offering you a guarantee that we are 100% serious about plugging all leaks."

"What guarantee?" Vero said.

Suddenly there was a popping noise and Hozumi slumped forward in his chair. A small plume of smoke curled out of his mouth and nostrils.

Vero gasped in shock.

"Sweet Ares!" Jones said, moving forward and putting his hand on the man's neck.

"Is he dead?" Betti gasped. "Oh my god!"

Jones nodded.

"Geez," I said. "Some guarantee."

"They must have triggered a device in his head," Vero said. "That is sick."

"Cold as ice," I said. "But an impressive guarantee."

"10 million to smoke some evil scientists," Jones said, turning to the rest of us. "I say we take it."

"We won't be getting most of that money," Vero said slowly, still staring at the dead man. "I'm sure we'll get paid well, but WDI is the one making the contract. It's not in our hands anyhow. Geez, though… I don't even know if I want to work with people like this."

"So long as we make a good cut," Jones said. "I'd work with the devil himself."

"Agreed," said Betti. "I like having toys like Elsie. She cost at least 10 mil all on her own."

"Well," I said. "Time to call Captain Williams."

I went upstairs. Zegal and Ward were playing some sort of a loud zombie shooting gallery game on the tri-D.

"Did you kill him, Tommy?" Ward said, pausing the game.

"No," I replied. "Someone else did."

"What do you mean?" Ward asked.

"I'll get back to you on that. I'm calling the captain."

"Roger," Ward said, restarting the game.

I went into my room and shut out the sound of moaning and explosions, then called the captain and gave him the lowdown on the situation.

"Do you want to do this mission, Falkland?" he asked after I'd explained everything.

"Absolutely," I said.

"With just six people and strict need-to-know?"

"Yessir," I said. "No problem. Six of us can clear a facility like that. Like a knife through butter. It's good money. And it's a chance to potentially stop a plague from being released. If you'd seen Heiermach die, you'd go by yourself to keep that from happening to anyone else."

He nodded. "Fine, then. I will contact THI and get back to you."

It only took about an hour before we received new orders. We were off to Gunwal.

Chapter 10

We were booked on a passenger liner to the Gunwal system. She took us to Mordas Prime, where we were met by a sealed shipping container full of supplies provided for the mission by WDI. Weapons, vacuum-ready battlesuits, I-128 ceramic frag grenades, MREs, explosive charges, surveillance gear and assorted devices and trinkets. A local shipping contractor watched the man on the gravlift unloading the equipment with a frown.

"What's the matter?" I asked, seeing the direction of his gaze.

"Union labor. They insist on offloading. Local regulations. We could do it ourselves using the ship's crew and it would cost a lot less." The man shook his head. "Costs twice as much and takes three times longer. Dealing with the local regs here is a nightmare."

"I'm sure," I said politely. *Though not as bad as reoccurring nightmares where you're under enemy fire trying to hold a friend's guts inside his body as he chokes to death on his own blood,* I almost added.

A tight-lipped THI rep escorted us to a nearby landing pad where a blocky Braun Freightliner K-series scientific transport awaited us. This one was a model often used to transport victims after major catastrophes. They had built in gel-tubes for stasis, multiple operating rooms and hermetic seals between every room, along with special ventilation systems. The last I'd seen of a few friends had been them being loaded into ships a lot like this one. You could haul out about 100 casualties on them, judging by the space inside. Usually they were reserved for the worst cases.

Not a good sign.

When we first stepped inside I could smell disinfectant and the plastic smell of instawrap bandaging. The brass plate by the door read "*St. Roch*," then the registration number, followed by *Besley MedCorp, Mordas Prime*. THI was leasing the vessel, so we had to assume they'd have at least two operators among the crew.

A crewman in a blue uniform welcomed us aboard and took us to the cafeteria. There were three stainless tables there. At one of them sat four men, also in blue uniforms, apparently having a quick conference. The crew. The men stood and one of them welcomed us. "You must be the investigative team," he said. "I'm Captain Teller. Welcome aboard."

"Thank you," Vero said.

"We're still waiting for the cleaning crew, captain," said the crewman who had brought us in.

"Let me know when they're on board, Adler," Teller said, dismissing the man. He looked back at Vero. "You guys can help yourselves to whatever you like in the cafeteria. It's not good but you'll probably live. Fortunately, if you get food poisoning or anything, the boys here are all EMT-certified." The guys in blue snickered as we laughed politely. "Adler is our gopher. If you need anything, you can get him on the com. You can pick our quarters as well. They're tight but not terrible. We're just wrapping up a quick meeting now. Feel free to get what you like and grab a table."

We headed over to the kitchen. I made my way over to the coffee machine at the counter and dialed up a cup.

"A cleaning crew?" Ward said.

"Probably a biohazard team," Jones said, as he dialed up a snack.

"Makes sense to me," I said, sipping the coffee. It tasted a little like disinfectant. I wondered if my nose was tricking me or if someone was actually cleaning the machine with the stuff. I added a little more cream to cover the taste.

Betti and Vero joined us by the coffee machine. The former had a small tray of freeze-dried celery sticks, with what looked like a dish of barbecue sauce, the latter had a fruit juice.

"THI already has their scientist on the ship," Vero said. "Now we're just waiting for the biohazard boys."

"Told you," Jones said to Ward around a mouthful of pretzel sticks.

"This guy has worked with some deadly stuff in the past," Betti said.

"The scientist?" Vero said.

"Dr. Aston Shutt is his name," Betti said. "He's on retainer with THI but his background is in military research and development. Word is he is "I am become death" class, whatever that means." Betti crunched down on a sauce-covered celery stick and shrugged.

"You drink all the coffee?" a voice said from behind me.

"That's him," Betti said around a mouthful of green stuff.

I turned to see a balding man with bushy black eyebrows and moved to let him get to the machine. He dialed in a cup of black coffee with three sugars.

"Dr. Shutt?" Vero said.

"In the flesh," he said, blowing on his coffee. "Who are you?"

"Veronique Parey, Wardogs Investigative Department," Vero replied. "This is my partner, Bettina Wolfsganger, and these four gentlemen–"

"Are the grunts," he interrupted. "Great. Good to meet you all, but my work isn't going to finish itself." He gave us a half-wave and stalked off with his coffee.

"Grunts," Jones said. "Nice."

"We fight so men like him can be free," Ward said piously.

"I'll free him of something," Zelag muttered.

We got our cabins situated. My cabin had a small desk, a bed with a mattress and a visiscreen linked to the ship's net. I would enjoy the space for the day and a half it took to reach our destination.

The biohazard guys showed up with their stuff a few hours after we arrived and we were now on our way to the asteroid. It was a black rock on a long, cold elliptical orbit around Gunwal's sun. I thought of Heiermach's death more than once and hoped to Ares we wouldn't have a repeat of that nastiness. What if the researchers figured out we were coming and flooded the airlock with the plague virus? It couldn't get through our vacuum suits, but what if we didn't decontaminate properly or something? What if we got in a firefight and a puncture let in that shit? I thought of Heiermach's disintegrating skin again. Geez. We should just nuke it. But no, this was simple enough. I'd killed more people in a few minutes than were on this entire station. We would certainly be given the station diagrams, plus the personnel manifest. And we'd have pressurized biohazard suits. Completely safe for us. Go in, secure the station, collect our bounty, then throw a few thousand more in the old retirement account. No problem.

But why did they need us to go inside? I pushed it out of my mind. My job wasn't to think.

After a good night's sleep—although there's no real day or night in space—I reviewed our orders again. We were supposed to enter the base and clear it, room to room, and escort Dr. Shutt through the facility. I decided to look up the base on the ship's net. As I expected, there was no data. I flipped it off and headed to the cafeteria for breakfast.

When I got there, I found I'd been beaten there by Betti and Ward. They were sitting at a table with their plates already. At another table sat two guys in gray jumpsuits with fluorescent bands on the arms, legs and torso. One had a ponytail, the other guy was older and graying. The cleanup crew.

I dialed in a coffee—with extra cream and sugar—and joined my people.

"Good morning," Betti said. "No breakfast for you?"

"Not yet," I said. "Coffee is more important."

Ward chewed a bite of waffle and nodded. "It tastes weird, though."

"Yeah," I said. "Like disinfectant."

"That's just your nose," Betti said.

"Maybe."

Vero walked in and waved to us, then dialed in her order. She came to the table with a bagel and a cup of tea.

"Sleep okay?" she asked us.

"I missed Tommy's snoring," Ward said. "The silence kept me up all night."

I sipped my coffee.

"You okay, Tommy?" Vero asked.

"I think going into this place is a lousy idea," I said. "Better to just burn it to cinders."

"I've had similar thoughts," Vero said.

"There isn't even a layout of the station on the ship's computers."

"No problem," Betti said. "I can hook you up."

"Good," I said. "At least we'll have an idea of what we're getting into."

Jones and Zelag walked in, laughing about something, then grabbed some grub and joined us.

"What's up?" Jones said, hacking into a sausage.

"Tommy and Vero don't like the idea of going into this base," Ward said.

"Scared of salamanders," Betti said.

"If you'd seen what happened to Heiermach on the skycar, salamanders would scare the space out of you," Zelag said. "I don't like it either."

"Come on," Jones said. "We'll have vacc suits. And if someone on the station releases that virus into the air, they'll die."

"Maybe they have a vaccine," Zelag said.

"Maybe," Jones said. "But still, our suits are made for space. A virus can't get in."

"They can tear," I said.

"They're tough and you know it. We'll be careful. Sheesh, Tommy, we've seen much worse stuff in the field. This is just another job."

"I don't know," said Vero. "It might be a trap."

"A trap?" Betti said. "Why?"

"To kill off all the witnesses to this thing," Vero said, pushing some scrambled eggs and greens around on her plate. "I don't like it. Remember, they killed the guy that told us about the job."

"Yeah, that was cold," Ward said.

"It's just their culture," Jones said. "He'd screwed up, so he had to make amends."

"Doesn't mean they don't think we're a problem to dispose of," I said. "Vero is used to investigating stuff. If she thinks something is off, I don't see any reason to doubt her."

"Ten mil, dude," Jones said. "And they hired us. Why hire us if they want us iced?"

"True," Ward said. "There are simpler ways to kill us. They could have gassed us in the safe house. Or we could have had an accident at the spaceport. This ship could have a bomb on it. They have loads of easier options."

"That's true," Betti said, chewing on a piece of toast. "And why hire a medical ship and a biohazard team?" She nodded her head towards the guys at the third table. "They know too much as well? They don't know anything."

"And the ship's crew," Jones said. "Getting more people involved just to kill them all—it doesn't make sense."

"You have a point," I said.

"You know," said Vero. "I'll bet there's something more going on here."

"What do you mean?" Zelag said.

Vero took a swig of her tea and made a strange face. "You know, I think this does have disinfectant in it." She set the mug down, leaned forward and clasped her hands together. "I'll tell you what I think. I think THI's agreement with this biotech company was compromised somehow. Something has gone wrong—really wrong—something beyond just not wanting to be associated with a bioweapons company. They need us to cover up something worse."

The biohazard guys got up and dumped their dishes, then came back to our table.

"Good day," said the one with the ponytail. "I'm Ted."

"And I'm Dave," said the graying man.

"Nice to meet you," I said.

"So, Wardogs, right?" Ted said.

"Yep," said Zelag. "You need anybody killed?"

"Um, no," said Ted, looking confused. "Nothing like that."

"Great," Zelag said. "Come back and talk to us when you do."

"Well," said Ted. "Okay, then."

They walked off, looking discombobulated. Jones laughed and slapped Zelag on the back. "Nice work, diplomat."

Betti laughed too. Vero just shook her head.

Dr. Shutt walked in and headed to the coffee maker. He poured a cup, then turned to leave.

"Doctor?" Vero said. "Sit down for a moment, would you?"

"I'm busy," he said, hesitating.

"Just give us a minute," she insisted.

"Fine," he said, taking a seat. "What's up?"

"You're supposed to go in with us, correct?" Vero said.

He nodded. "Yes, which is why I should be working on my research right now."

"Because things have headed south in a big way?" I said.

He looked around nervously. "Well, I…"

"Tell us what's up," Vero said. "Why can't we just nuke this rock and call it a day?"

Shutt took a nervous swig from his coffee.

"Tell us," I said. "We know this virus is evil as hell. We saw it kill a man. THI has hired us to take out whoever is cooking up this stuff, but going cabin-to-cabin isn't necessary. Can you give us one good reason why we shouldn't blow the place up instead?"

"I really shouldn't say anything," Shutt said as he tried to stand.

"Yes, you should say something," Zelag said, putting his hand on the doctor's arm and pulling him back down. Shutt tried to pull away but found the man's grip irresistible.

"The grunts are restless," Vero said with a charming smile. "Listen. It would be better if you just let us know why we have to go in. We're going to see whatever is happening anyway, so you're not going to tell us anything we won't eventually find out on our own."

The doctor sighed and drained his coffee. "Fine. Let's just say there may have been a breach we need to secure."

"The virus is loose on the station?" Betti said, eyes widening.

"No, no, nothing like that," the doctor said. "I mean, I hope not. But there's a possibility that the virus was already taken off the rock by bad actors."

"We know that," Vero said. "It was used to kill Heiermach."

"Yes," Shutt said. "But that was a designer version of the strain. It was almost certainly a test, and it was also directly DNA targeted. But we suspect someone inside the company may have already smuggled more samples off the asteroid. What if they're selling it to someone? We need to find out what is there, what isn't, and who they sold it to."

"Geez, doc," Jones said. "You're saying the version that killed Heiermach wasn't virulent? Looked pretty damn virulent to us when he was puking blood on the floor with his skin erupting in boils."

"You were there?" Shutt said.

"Damn straight," Jones said.

"And yet you lived," Shutt said, as if this proved something.

"So?" Jones said.

"You'd be dead if the full version of this virus had gotten out. As would most of the population of Feymanus."

"Wait a minute," Ward said. "They could kill that many people with this stuff?"

"Absolutely," said the doctor. "We know it got out of the lab in at least the modified form, or perhaps it was just the isolated toxin, we don't know. What if the complete version made it off? One of the employees must have sold the modified version to someone or your CEO client wouldn't be dead. This is why we need to do a little research in there instead of blowing the whole thing to pieces. Do you understand?"

"I see," said Vero. "This is making more sense now."

"Yes," said the doctor. "But don't worry about catching the virus. It's highly unlikely that anyone released it on the station. These people know what they're doing."

"Though it could already be off the rock and in the hands of a criminal organization," Zelag said.

"Or a hostile government," Betti added.

"Or the Unity," I said, feeling sick.

"Hence THI's need to shut this thing down before they're linked to it," Vero said.

The doctor said nothing, but the look on his face told us we'd hit the crux of it. "Now you understand why this is so important. It can't get out."

"We don't intend to let it," Vero assured him.

Jones let the doctor go and he left us alone to ponder the situation.

"Well," Ward said. "Looks like we're going to have to earn our pay again."

"No worries. In and out," Jones said. "They're just a bunch of science dorks. It'll be like shooting fish in a barrel."

Asteroid 30193 G-S hung in space, looking like a million others I'd seen. Put it in a lineup and I couldn't spot it again. Captain Teller hailed the base multiple times but there was no response.

"Is this the right asteroid?" Ward said as we stood on the bridge and watched the rock slowly rotate.

"Yes sir," said the navigator from behind him. "30193 G-S."

"They're playing possum," Vero said. "Heat and oxygen, but no signs of life."

"I have no idea what's going on here," said the Captain. "The base is inside the rock. They haven't been supplied in a few weeks and I was told by THI that they would be expecting a shipment. We're using the code we were supplied but we're getting nothing."

"Well," I said. "Time to go wake them up."

Twenty minutes later I stood in St. Roch's airlock with Jones, Zelag and Ward. We were suited up and carried our PN60 rifles, along with plenty of I-128 ceramic frags. I was carrying a Cerberus as a backup, while Ward had enough explosive charges in his bag to blow up three asteroids. According to the manifest we'd gotten from THI, there were only 28 people in residence on the station. A station master, a chief engineer, a maintenance guy, a couple of techs to keep everything working, a secretary, a chief scientist and a project manager, plus 20 researchers. We weren't too worried about them. They were civilians. And under Ascendancy regs, they were all declared capital criminals. Fair game.

"Remember, your orders are to shoot on sight," Vero said over our coms as the docking tunnel clanked into place.

"Copy that," I replied. We'd been over this before. Our job was to make 28 corpses, then Dr. Shutt would board the station along with Vero and Betti. The latter had added the station layout to our suit computers so we'd be going in with eyes open.

St. Roch's airlock hissed open and we headed into the tunnel. Once we were clear, our ship's airlock snapped to a close. Ward popped open the access terminal on the station's airlock and scanned a chip card. There was a pause while Elsie hacked the lock through the link. We held our rifles at the ready, waiting to engage. My heart pounded and I felt the buzz of blood in my ears. My adrenal system was telling me it was time to kick ass.

Tick… tick… tick… the seconds moved by. *WHOOSH!* The door opened and we looked into blackness. Our visuals switched through the spectrums, but still there were no signs of life.

Jones and Ward rushed through, rifles at the ready, followed by Zelag and I. According to my readouts, fresh air was circulating. In front of us was a blast door, also closed. Ward popped open the terminal to let Elsie crack it.

"Eyes on," I ordered. This door opened faster, leading into another room. Still nothing on the thermals, and the lights were off here as well. I looked around. Something was not right. We were in a foyer of some sort with open doors leading in multiple directions. My suit computer laid out the design of the station and overlaid our team's symbols on the map.

"We'll go to the bridge," I said. "If there's anyone here, at least someone should be there."

A hallway to the left led us deeper into the asteroid. There were doors on both sides, most of them shut. Still no sign of people.

"Where the hell is everyone?" Jones said. "It's vacant!"

"Good question," I replied. "Keep moving. The bridge is close." We reached the command center and the door opened automatically, no hacking required. We entered a medium-sized room with a few computer terminals. Empty.

"Vero, we've reached the bridge," I reported. "No resistance. No nothing. Heat is on, atmo is on, lights are off."

"You don't see anyone at all?" Betti said over the com. "Everyone should be there. The last visit in THI's records showed a full complement."

"Maybe they abandoned ship," Ward said. "Someone must have tipped them off."

"Check the computer," Vero said. "See if you can find the station master's log."

"Roger," I said. "Jones and Zelag, seal the perimeter and guard the doors. Ward and I will take a look."

I woke the terminal in front of me, Ward at my side.

"I know this system," he said. "It's a Mark 37. Touchscreen, heavy on the icons." On the screen were displayed various boxes. He tapped through them rapidly and found the station master's log. The last entry was more than a week ago. My sense that something was seriously wrong began to ping more insistently.

"Pull it up from the last recorded delivery," I said.

"When was that?" Ward said.

"3403.215," Betti replied.

He pulled up the datestamp on the log and we began to read.

1723 Hours, 3403.215: *Scheduled delivery arrived on freighter Old Salt at 1335 hours. Dr. Sesstal requests more growth medium, but otherwise stocked for the quarter. Auto meals still disappointing—must put in request for better assortment. Dr. Smithson claimed she quote felt under the weather unquote and was not present in lab today. Caulfield also took long break mid-afternoon during ship unload. Perhaps should request better recreational equipment for gym to relieve monotony. Darts?*

1154 Hours, 3403.216: *Mortten says unhappy with Smithson's work in lab, mostly seems to be personality conflicts.*

2025 Hours, 3403.218: *Dealt with small air leak in laboratory and had to clear researchers for half a day. Damage repaired by Caulfield. Caulfield reports seal breakage likely due to shifting of rubble created during facility construction. Caulfield and Dr. Smithson spending more time together.*

1935 Hours, 3403.219: *Amusing incident regarding autochef's attempt at lasagna for staff dinner—most everyone there to witness the mess. Cheered us up.*

2021 Hours, 3403.220: *Dr. Carson reported inability to find certain samples. Claims samples were placed in deep freeze ten days ago. Carson reports when he went to add more samples today, previous were gone. Checked log but no record of previous samples. Carson insists they were there but now gone. Ordered a search of computers by Layton but still no entry found. Freezer should have recorded access upon placement and if removed—no evidence of either. Also nothing on security footage. Stress must be getting to Carson. Have considered requesting more videos for station library. Uplifting, inspirational—no more horror or scary films.*

1945 Hours, 3403.221: *More tension among scientists. Smithson made case Carson is losing samples. Personal note: music can be therapy. Read about this long ago: play nice songs for plants, they live. Dark music can kill. Plan: play soft music through station. Could bring more peace. Spent several hours searching library for good choices but not sure if implementation might be seen as me trying to intervene in personal mind space of staff. Still, food for thought.*

1833 Hours, 3403.222: *Watching cameras around ship as precaution after supposed sample loss, but have seen nothing amiss as of yet, other than Caulfield and Smithson carrying on long conversation in hall. Caulfield is definitely sweet on Smithson. Carson still defiant and claims memory is fine and that Caulfield was in the lab by himself fixing leak at time samples disappeared. Yet Carson is oldest researcher on station. Very agitated. Told him I did not care about personal feelings but tried to follow book, he said quote damn the book, I know what I put where and when endquote. Wonder if touched a nerve. Nervous system is very delicate. Many wires running through the body from the brain, all highly attuned.*

2221 Hours, 3403.223: *Base of reasoning is in fact the gut. Almost like a second brain. What one eats highly influential on behavior. Note reaction of body to eating heavy carb load meal. Sleepiness. Sugar can lead to agitation*—little bugs going nuts in there!

1331 Hours, 3403.224: *Karsten very upset over note I put in galley on keeping healthy. Says he feels targeted because I asked him about his diet and questioned intake of sugar. Karsten is overweight. Told him addictions are unhealthy and affect us all. Asked Layton again this afternoon about kitchen arrangements and argued that fire not an issue. Used by man for a million years. Working on personal projects to keep satisfied. Skin itches.*

2224 Hours, 3403.224: *Feel like I'm being followed.*

1513 Hours, 3403.225: *Skin still an issue. Whitman noticed. Told her hermetic environment causes lack of exposure to natural world, putting the human immune system into hypersensitive state maybe about allergies, but I shared I have no history of such. Can manifest in adulthood, she said so funny to me will fix later when money arises told her May also be stress.*

2021 Hours, 3403.225: *Listened to robert DiIanni syntar nocturnes for one hour this evening so beautiful. considered playing through coms but resisted urge. shall not force personal relaxation on others peace must be sought, not imposed roger roger roger roeger*

0834 Hours, 3403.226: *and now its bugs*

1219 Hours, 3403.226: *doors may open and close into parallel spaces and what we see is not all there is. Special apce where I hang my hat so to speak*

2037 Hours, 3403.227: *Medicine dOES NOT equire consent of recipient to healing for body and this is to the soul. The soul cANNOT BE measured but weight can be removed through beauty. NOTHING MORE WoNDutiful than voices lifted up in harmony 0 oh choir music always favorite, listen liten on*

2310 Hours, 3403.227: *everything has happened badly now s om uc cutt bolood Why me???*

0934 Hours, 3403.228: *apnts se of unnatural lights causde tension now all gone ALL GONE ALGON ad me alone in the dark here tO?NGIT lost souls not all lone tho still*

1239 Hours, 3403.228: *bovious eye MUST BE recent dev in evolution to history. Cannot see me now tho still npt sur.*

1703 Hours, 3403.228: *darkness is in the womb note nothing cacan be more comforting. PEACE OF Thhe womb—stay alerte will all deiver when arrives*

0134 Hours, 3403.229: *cant remove skin without painpainpain is blood leaving the body*

2234 Hours, 3403.229: *so is hIDE AD N SEEK NOW HA!*

"That's it," Ward said. "Last entry was a week ago. What the hell was all that?"

"It sounds as if he was having a psychotic break," Betti commented thoughtfully. "But why didn't anyone notice?"

"I guess we'll have to find out," I said calmly. But inside my suit, my skin was crawling.

Chapter 11

"Can you see life forms at all on the scans?" I asked.

"No," Betti replied over the com. "That rock is full of magnetite and heavy metals. From out here we've got nothing."

"We're coming over with Dr. Shutt," Vero said. "Maybe Betti can get something from inside."

"Roger," I replied. They'd seen the station logs thanks to the visor cams on my and Ward's suits, yet they still wanted to join us. Couldn't knock them on courage, that's for sure. All I wanted at this point was to get out. The silence was oppressive and the station master's log had given me the creeps.

"Jones, Zelag, go to the airlock. The doc and the girls are on their way," I said.

"Roger," came Jones's voice. "Any luck on the computer?"

"One of the crew and a scientist were in on something together," I said. "Looks like they used a leak in the lab to cover for stealing samples."

"And the station master went full psycho," Ward added.

"Yeah, that too," I said.

"I'm gonna go psycho myself if we have to keep hanging around a dead space station," Jones said. "See you in a few."

"It's like one of those ghost ships," Ward said. "Traveling the void, piloted by AIs, with no one alive on board."

A few minutes later, Betti, Vero and the doc joined us, escorted in by Jones and Zelag. Both the women had donned vacc battlesuits. It was the first time I'd seen Betti suited up. All 5'3" of her. She looked cute in a suit, but I knew that even a small woman like her made for a formidable weapon thanks to the suit's powered exoskeleton.

Betti jacked into the ship's computer, then frowned. "I'm not getting anything on the internal sensors either."

"Then we'll have to do things the old-fashioned way," Ward said, giving his Popov-Norinco an affectionate pat.

"Let's make a speed run through and see what we can find," I said. After reading the station master's log, I had the terrible feeling that we were going to find nothing but bodies. "In and out. I'm not keen to hang around a plague manufacturing facility any longer than I have to."

"I'll bet they're all crowded into one room, hanging from the ceiling like bats or something," Zelag said.

"No," Jones said. "They're zombies. This is what we spend all our rec time practicing for, right? Let's shoot some zombies!"

"All right, enough," I said. I turned to Dr. Shutt. "Tell me, doc. What would make the station master go nuts like that?"

"Could be stress," he replied. "Though guys with his level of responsibility are usually even keel. Bureaucratic minds. Could be a tainted atmosphere. Or he could just be genetically susceptible to mental illness. The human mind is a fragile and mysterious device."

"What about the virus?" I asked. "Could it have been released on the ship?"

"I doubt it," he replied. "But I'm not taking my helmet off either, no matter what the sensors say. I don't see anyone here, so it's clear that something is seriously amiss."

"Would the virus make people go nuts?" I asked. "I mean, Heiermach just died—he didn't act crazy first."

"No, no chance. If it were the virus, the station master would succumb to the infection before developing aberrant mental symptoms. In layman's terms, the plague virus release the toxin in sufficiently lethal quantities that the victim does not enjoy the luxury of going insane before his demise."

"So what happened?" I asked.

"Could it be a fractional exposure," Betti said.

"To the virus?" the doctor scoffed. "No. Even a small sample would replicate too rapidly inside the body."

"Not the virus," said Vero. "The toxin the virus produces. Betti researched it. It's hallucinogenic in very small doses. The salamander toxin."

"Yes," said the doctor. "This is true, according to what we've read from indigenous Achenaran shamans. In infitesimal amounts. But the only way you'd get exposed to that is if you were perhaps growing the virus on a medium under less-than-optimal conditions and perhaps got some of the used medium... but even then... hmm." The doctor tried to stroke his chin, forgetting he was wearing a pressure suit, then continued. "I don't know. I will have to think on that. But now we need to get into the main lab computers, if possible," Dr. Shutt said. "I want to dump everything onto my own drive for analysis and see if we can figure out what's missing."

"Agreed," said Betti. "That's a priority."

"Okay, Falkland," Vero said. "Let's all go to the lab first, then worry about finding everyone," Vero said.

"No," I said. "It's not necessary to all go together. If we want to get out of here sooner rather than later, we should split into two teams."

"I'm fine with that," Vero said. "Betti should definitely go to the lab with Dr. Shutt, though. I'm willing to join the search party if it gets us out of here faster.

"Good," I said. "I'll take Zelag, Betti and the doc to the lab as Team Red, so Team Blue is you, Jones and Ward. Start with the sleeping quarters. Let's move."

We left the bridge in one group for the first leg, as the main hallway headed towards both the lab and the dormitories. I kept scanning as we went but didn't see any targets. We travelled through a long hallway to a central hub with benches, reclining chairs and a few wilting potted plants. Above was a sun dome, currently set on a sleep setting of scattered stars. There was obviously some money blown on this facility. The feeling of the station was getting to me. It was dark but clean, everything seemed to be in place, but no one was home. There were no signs of struggle, no blood, not even a knocked over table or a spilled glass on the floor. It was like everyone checked out for an evening on the town—but there was no town for 20 billion kilometers.

I hated it. Give me a hot and heavy battlefield over this creepshow any day. It was like a freaking haunted house, only out in the lonely depths of space. But you're in charge this time, Tommy, I reminded myself. They're looking to you. No pressure.

"To the left is the hallway that leads down into the lab area. Eating facilities, gym and dormitories off to the right," Betti said. I could see the same layout inside my visor so her report was unnecessary. We split our teams at that fork and wished each other luck.

Getting to the laboratory was more trouble than I'd expected. There were series of locks and decontamination rooms we had to get through, requiring Betti and Elsie to hack their way through multiple entries. She reset the locks so they'd open automatically for us next time. And every new door that suddenly opened had us on edge, to the point that we were all getting trigger-happy.

We made it to the lab without incident and without any clues as to what had happened. The lab itself was more of a cluster of laboratory rooms, along with a small cafeteria and a conference room. In the work areas there was a bunch of scientific equipment I knew nothing about and definitely did not want to touch. We went through the rooms quickly, assuring they were all clear, then got Betti and the doc set up on the main computer terminal.

"Maybe the staff got word we were coming for them," Zelag said as we watched the doors. "Maybe they were all in on it, and they had an executive inside THI. Then they might have taken off without anyone knowing about it."

"Maybe," I said. I doubted it. They would have taken their gear. This stuff had to be expensive.

"They could have cleared out of here and took their plague with them."

"I don't know," I said honestly. "If the Ascendancy got wind of this place they'd be toast. Where would they run?"

"Maybe another government had an agent here," Zelag said.

"Like the Unity?" I asked. There was an ugly thought. I glared at the computers suspiciously.

"I was thinking one of the independent planets."

"Bingo," Dr. Shutt announced. "The books are most definitely cooked."

"How?" I asked.

"Betti's AI friend can explain more readily, I'm sure."

Betti stared into space for a few seconds, then spoke. "There was some sort of an accident in the lab. The research log was shut off, then some things were reset. Warnings were disabled and a few samples disappeared from the record. There are fewer tubes now in storage than before the accident."

"How many fewer?"

"Looks like about 10 percent of the virus is missing," Betti said.

"Damn," Zelag said.

"Is that a lot?" I asked.

"It's more than enough," Dr. Shutt said. "All you really need to recreate this thing is one virus. Evidence suggests that they removed multiple sequences. They stole enough to run their own lab outside of this one, that's for sure."

"What does that mean, practically speaking?" I asked.

"It means that they have enough to launch a plague, plus recreate this virus from the ground up," Betti said.

"Tommy," my com crackled. The signal was bad due to the heavy metals surrounding the station but I could still identify the voice as Vero's. "Are you almost done over there?"

"Roger that, Parey," I said, looking at Betti and the doc. "You have everything you need?" I asked.

"Yes," said the doctor, patting his portable drive. "We have it all."

"We're good here," I reported back to Vero.

"Good," she said. "You really need to get over here right now."

"Everything okay?" I asked.

"Not really," she said.

"Clarify," I responded.

"We're fine," came her voice. There was a hint of fear in it. No, not just fear. Terror. "But…"

"But what?" I said.

"We found the crew."

A woman lay on her bed in a nightgown, a hole burned between her breasts.

"Laser," Ward said clinically. "Right in the heart. Angle indicates she was lying down and the shooter was standing near the doorway. She was probably asleep, never knew what hit her."

"That's horrible," Betti said, looking at the body.

"No, that's lucky," Ward corrected her.

The woman on the bed was fifty-something with cropped gray hair. She was plump, with the pasty look of a woman who had spent most of her life indoors.

"Who is she?" I asked.

"Kersley Whitman," Betti reported. "This is her cabin."

"There are two sets of quarters," Jones said. "We're in the dormitories for the researchers right now. There's a separate, smaller set of quarters for the crew. The two hallways meet up at a little recreational hub and don't connect directly."

"And you found bodies in both wings?" I asked.

"Yeah," said Jones. "Someone has made our job easier."

"Don't be too sure," Vero said. "We're still short six."

"You've already ID'ed the bodies?" I asked.

"Yeah," she said. "All 22 of them. This is seriously messed up."

I looked at the woman on the bed and felt zero sympathy for her. She'd been making viruses that could destroy entire worlds. The galaxy was better off without her.

"Messed up that they're dead?" I said.

"Hell, no," Vero replied. "These people deserved it if anyone ever did. I'll show you what's messed up, just follow me."

I did and we moved a couple rooms down and pushed open the door. The locks were all off, thanks to Elsie.

On the bed lay a balding man in scrubs. Two small holes were burned through his chest.

"Another murder," I said. "So?"

"So?" Vero said. "Look at his feet."

"He's wearing shoes," I said.

"Exactly," Vero replied. "Dr. Gim here is wearing shoes. Whitman was in her nightgown, probably killed in her sleep. The doctor was killed when he was awake. He's been placed on the bed."

"The angle of entry is different. Two shots as well," Ward said. "Our killer hit him twice. He might have been moving when he was shot."

"Yes," said Vero.

"Roll him over," I said. I had a hunch.

Jones pushed the guy over on the bed. I heard the sound of escaping gasses and I was glad my battlesuit filtered the air. It must have stunk something fierce. The holes on the dead man's back leaked fluid and they were larger than those in the front. "Shot from behind," Jones said. "The laser burned in and through."

"There are more like this," Vero said. "In both the crew cabins and the scientists' rooms we saw there were some killed in their sleep and some who were almost certainly murdered elsewhere, then dragged back to their rooms."

"According to the records, this is his assigned cabin," Betti said, again from the door.

"Yes," said Vero. "We checked on that already. Every corpse was put back in his own room and laid on his own bed."

"Why?" Ward said. "They're dead. Who cares?"

"A psychopath would care," Betti said.

"Exactly," Vero nodded. "Someone liked to be neat and precise, dotting their T's and crossing their I's."

"Other way around," Zelag corrected her.

"Oh, of course," Vero said with a nervous laugh. "I haven't seen something like this since I had to work on a series of killings in an exo refugee settlement, back before I started with Wardogs."

"Well," I said. "Where's our killer?"

"I don't know," Vero said. "He could be one of the dead. Or one of the six."

"Do the six survivors include the man and the woman the station manager was concerned about in his log?" I asked.

"Dr. Kara Smithson and Gavin Caulfield," Betti said.

"No. They weren't among the dead," Vero said. "Neither was the station master."

"Everett Case," Betti said.

"So what happened?" Ward said. "Somebody killed 20 people, then disappeared?"

"The remaining six could be in league with each other," Jones said.

"I dunno," Ward said. "The station master was worried about Caulfield and Smithson."

"But he was crazy," Vero said. "What if he's out there watching us right now?"

"Out where?" Zelag said.

"He's probably dead too," Ward said. "My bet is the two thieves whacked him and the other three, then left. Or something like that."

"One way to find out," Jones said.

"Agreed," I said. "We've only covered the station. Time to check out the rest."

Chapter 12

We split into two teams again. Vero, Jones and Ward headed for the galley while Betti, Zelag and I hit the cargo bay.

We walked down the hallway and then took a set of stairs upwards to the cargo bay. There was an industrial elevator that went up and down but I sure as heck wasn't going to take my team into a box like that, not without knowing what was up with the survivors. The stairs took longer but were the right choice.

We reached the cargo bay in about ten minutes. It was closer to the surface of the asteroid than the rest of the station, with the exception of the airlock we'd entered from the *St. Roch*.

The cargo bay was dark like the rest of the place, its entrance airlock a gaping mouth. We moved in and I looked up to see the large cargo doors above us. According to my diagram, there was an uneven meter or so of the asteroid's metallic surface covering the top of the doors so they couldn't be readily seen unless opened to receive cargo. Massive arms were folded up inside the bay. It looked like they would accordion out and pick up the entire door like a huge roof, probably folding back far enough so a ship could simply land in the center of the room. As we moved slowly into the bay and fanned out, I saw lighting strips on the floor, now dark, obviously there to guide landing craft.

Around the edges of the room were tanks and cargo containers, a forklift and tools, various crates and supplies, but there were still no signs of life. Everything was gray on my thermals except the power conduits and piping. We moved slowly and thoroughly from container to container, popping the seals and looking inside each one.

The tap of our boots on the floor echoed eerily and I kept think-ing I heard things I didn't. I wondered if we were being watched. The pulse of blood in my veins told me to run or fight but there was no one to fight. Nothing but random cargo in a big empty room.

Vero's voice came over my com and I jumped. "Tommy, we've found something else. Something really bad."

"Spill it," I said. By Possenti, she made me jumpy when she did that. Just say it, woman!

"Two more bodies," she said, a slight quaver in her voice.

"Okay, then we're up to 22," I said, projecting calm. "That's good."

"No," she said. "These are different. Oh God…"

"Just spit it out, dammit," I snapped.

There was a brief silence, then Ward's voice came over the comm. "We found two bodies in the galley freezer, Falkland. Caulfield and Smithson," Ward said. "Well, we found most of two bodies. There are parts missing."

"Parts missing?" I repeated, thinking I'd misheard him.

"Affirmative," he said. "Smithson is missing a leg up to the knee. Caulfield is sans an arm."

"They get shot off?" I asked.

"No," he replied. "They look like they were cut off. Carved, actu-ally."

Carved?

"We also found what we think might be… leftovers."

"Leftovers?" I said. "You don't mean?"

"Yeah, uh… I think someone was kind of–"

"There's a damn cannibal on board!" Vero yelled in our ears. "Some-one butchered these people, made a meal of them, and took the time to pack away a plate of goddamn leftovers."

"Okay, okay," I replied, trying to get a grip on what they were telling me. "Don't freak out. We're coming to you now. We've found nothing."

I keyed off my mic and looked at Zelag. He was silent, but his eyes were wide. Betti's silver eyes were blank, she was off communing with the digital gods again.

"Let's go through the rest of the containers on the left wall, then get out of here," I said. "We need to rejoin the others. Vero sounds like she's about to lose it."

I turned to Betti. "You doing okay?"

"Yes, I'm all right," she nodded. "Elsie monitors my system, and judging by how weirdly calm I am, I think she just injected me with about a year's worth of calm-down chemicals."

"Good," I said, envying her. "But if Elsie starts to get nervous, let me know."

I'm sure I was a little paler than usual myself, though there's no way in hell I'd admit the creeping horror I was feeling to the others. This wasn't a good place for any of us and I wished we could simply blow up the joint and get the hell *OUT!*

There were three containers left. The first two contained chemicals and various lab equipment. The second was full of hardware and what appeared to be unassembled metal racks. The third one was full of food. This one had free-dried pre-fab packets on racks down both sides, leading to the end. I stepped inside and walked down the center. Vegetable stew. Yeast cakes in sauce. Lasagna with meat substitute. Everything looked normal to me. I pulled out a box and dropped it on the floor, then looked inside. Exactly as labelled. No severed limbs or boxes marked "human flesh". Always a good sign. I put it back on the rack and walked a little farther in, and then I saw that the back of the container looked to be wide open.

"Zelag," I said. "There's something off here."

I zoomed my vision and looked into the darkness. It was definitely deeper than the container itself. There was some sort of a tunnel continued off through the wall of the container and the cargo bay. Zelag followed my look.

"Oh, hell no!" he said.

"What is it?" Betti said.

"We've got a hidden tunnel here," I replied. It reminded me of the tunnels I'd seen on Macheeda back before I joined Wardogs and was just a grunt. They'd been built by pleasure-jack smugglers hiding from the local law. Long, grimy, dark passages, sometimes leading into opulent hidden apartments, sometimes into waste storage pits. But that was on a planet. What where they doing on an asteroid?

I keyed my com. "Blue Team, this is Falkland."

"We hear you," Vero replied.

"We've discovered a tunnel here, one that leads into the asteroid itself. We're going to check it out. We will be in contact again in no longer than thirty minutes, over."

"Be careful, Tommy," Vero said. "We've found something else."

Oh geez. "What is it?" I replied. There was another hesitation, then Ward broke in. "We found some bones," he said softly.

"Wonderful," I said. "Where?"

"Jones and I were doing a more intensive search and Vero had the idea that more remains might have been added to the incinerator. I figured it would have been ejected into space by whoever killed the people here. I was wrong. We found the bones there. Human. Pretty torched, but I'd say they match up to the bodies in the freezer. Leg bones."

"Roger," I replied. "We'll join you after we take a look inside the tunnel."

"No!" Vero said. "Let's just get out of here."

"I definitely don't want to hang around here either," Ward said.

"Copy that," Jones said, joining them on the comm. "Let's blow this place right the hell out of space and say goodbye."

There were few ideas that pleased me more at that point. My skin was crawling like crazy as I looked into the dark tunnel in front of me. Instead of agreeing, I turned to Zelag. "What do you say? I think we need to go in there."

"Yeah," he said. "I'm just concerned about getting out again."

"We need to take the data back to the ship," Betti insisted. "We could just set charges, then go back."

"Please, Tommy," Vero begged over the comm. "For God's sake, let's get the hell out of here. Dammit, there are chewed-up, carved-up bodies in the freezer! There are dead people killed in their sleep! What do you think you're going to find in those tunnels anyhow? Let's get the hell out of here! Now!"

It was then that I knew what I needed to do. The panicked reaction was never the right one. I wanted to leave the station just as bad as anyone, but I was had my orders and I had my mission. I was a Wardog. We didn't run from sick freaks no matter what they ate. People ran from us, not the other way around. The hysteria in Vero's voice didn't convince me to run, but to the contrary, it convinced me to stay.

Lo, though I walk though the station of the shadow of Death, I will fear no evil, because we are the baddest and best-armed bastards in the vicinity.

"Vero, settle down," I said. "We're Wardogs. We have a job. We came here to find out what happened to a virus capable of killing entire worlds. I sure as hell am not going to leave until we know the whole story. We have a contract. I'm not breaking it. And you aren't either."

There was a silence, then Jones's voice. "All right, Tommy, I'm in."

"I still like the nuke option," said Ward.

"We don't have one," Zelag pointed out. "Falkland is right. We need to do this right."

"I think–" Vero said, but I cut her off.

"It's not your call, Parey," I said. "First, shut up and take a deep breath. Now, tell me as an investigator, if you were looking at this situation from the outside, what would you advise we do next?"

There was a pause and I heard her exhale sharply. Her voice was calmer when she spoke again. "I would recommend we check out the tunnel and see if the station master is in there. He's the primary suspect at this point."

"Good," I said. "So let's get it done, then we'll get out of here. We'll check out the tunnel, then join you. Falkland out."

I turned to my team. "Betti, you stay between Zelag and me. Zelag will take point, I'll cover the rear. If we tell you to get down, do it fast. Let's go."

With the boxes out of the way, it was easy to step onto the second shelf and then down again into the tunnel.

"These walls were cored with a driller," Zelag said, looking at the pattern of scraping grooves in the hard metal of the asteroid.

"Yeah, not natural," I agreed, running my gloved hand over the marks. "Not a drilling laser either."

About four meters deep, the tunnel ended abruptly at an airlock door. It looked jury-rigged, with a thick crust of hardened sealant around its edges. Betti opened it and we stepped into the small chamber on the other side, closed the first door, then popped the second door. It opened with a hiss and we stepped through. The tunnel ahead of us was long and we saw multiple dark openings on both sides.

"Whoa," Zelag said. "This is crazy!"

"Pay attention," I said as we moved in. "We'll go straight to wherever this one ends. Where are you both on oxygen?"

"8.2 hours," Zelag said.

"8.9," Betti replied.

I had 8.5 myself, according to my visor display. All the time in the world.

Zelag reached the first opening. It was on the right. He held up his hand and took a look, then put his hand down.

"Nothing down there," he said. "Empty."

Betti moved past next, followed by myself. It was dark and the tunnel stretched far off into the asteroid—and I could see other side passages along its length. Someone had done a lot of tunneling in this rock. I saw Zelag reach another entrance, this time on the left. "Clear," he said a moment later and moved past. As I passed I looked into that passage and noted it took a turn a few meters down.

After about ten minutes of passing empty hallways and still not reaching the end of the current tunnel, I began to realize the futility of the task.

"There is too much ground to cover," Betti said over the com. "I just had Elsie run the numbers on the passages we've seen so far. She estimates there could easily be more ten times more square meters inside these tunnels than in the station proper."

"We need to work smarter, not harder," Zelag said, looking down yet another long passage.

"What do you mean?" I asked.

"Chances are they're getting their oxygen from inside the station. These tunnels are all vacuum."

"Right," I said. "And?"

"That means they need to go back into the station now and again," Betti said. "They probably come back in for oxygen and supplies every so often."

"Good point," I said, suddenly having an idea. "Motion detectors. We could plant motion detectors at the entrance to the tunnel, and here and there around the station, then go back to the ship and wait for them to get tripped. We'd know right where they were. If we move fast, we can catch them resupplying."

"Sounds good to me," Zelag said. In front of us the tunnel continued and there were still more entrances to go. "A lot better than getting lost in here, anyhow."

"Yeah," I said. "Let's get back. I know we have some detectors in all that gear they sent with us."

I keyed in Blue Team. "Blue Team, this is Falkland."

"This is Parey," came the reply.

"The tunnels are too extensive to search. We've got another plan. We're headed to your position."

"Oh good!" Vero said, a little too enthusiastically, then corrected herself. "I mean, roger."

We started moving back through the tunnel, then Zelag hissed at me over the com as he looked down a side corridor. "Falkland, I'm getting something on the thermals here. Looks like a room off the hall, maybe."

I got beside him along the wall and looked down. Not a body, just a slightly warm patch down the tunnel, little more than a bare hint of thermal radiation. "Great," I said. "We must have missed that on the way in."

"Not much of a signature," Zelag observed.

"What is it?" Betti said.

"Probably a doorway," Zelag said. "Someone must have built an area under pressure and temp control. We're probably seeing a little of of that leaking into the passage."

I called in to Blue Team. "Blue Team, we're investigating an anomaly. Sit tight."

"Roger, Red," came Ward's voice. "Watch your back."

I nodded at Zelag and we moved down the hall. As suspected, we found an airlock door. Betti opened it quickly—it was empty! We stepped inside, guns at the ready, then listened as the air hissed in. If someone was here, we'd be ready.

SWISH! The second door opened and we found ourselves looking at the chaos of a work room. There were buckets and tanks, dirty work tables with mugs and plates on them, heating elements, tools, lab equipment, plus multiple vats of fluids. The room was quite warm according to my suit sensors—but no occupants, that we could see.

"That's a centrifuge," Betti announced, pointing to a piece of equipment to the right. "And there are freezers here, too. And I'm seeing petri dishes. Oh," she said suddenly. "This is almost certainly a bioweapons laboratory. Elsie says it's not secure at all, though."

"Wonderful," I said. "As if bioweapons alone aren't bad enough. Get this recorded and have her do an analysis of everything. Dr. Shutt should have a look at this."

"This is strange," Zelag said, picking up a plate of moldy food. "They really let this place go."

"Maybe they were losing their minds," I said. "Let's see if there's anything else to see."

We moved slowly around the back of the room to where two more doors were set in the wall. One of them opened into a bathroom with rigged-up shower facilities. I say it was a bathroom, but it was more of a bucket toilet with another bucket of water with a tap over a sink for hand washing. A grungy bar of soap sat on the counter, plus a cup with a couple of toothbrushes.

The other door opened into a dirty apartment. A few cots were along the back wall and there was a pile of dirty clothing on the floor. A box in one corner supported a chipped tri-D screen. Food wrappers were scattered about. Still no people, but it felt like we were getting warmer.

"Okay," I said after we'd ensured there was nothing else to see. "At least we know where they were hiding. We need to get back to our others. We'll have Shutt look at the footage and see what he thinks was going on here."

I keyed my com. "Sit tight, Blue Team. We're on our way. No contact."

"We'll be here," came Ward's voice.

We made our way out and shut the airlock behind us, then travelled back to the cargo bay without incident.

I looked around the huge room and noted the presence of multiple large oxygen tanks I had overlooked before. Yeah, anyone living back in those tunnels would probably get air there, plus they could help themselves to the food in the containers. Somebody, or multiple somebodies was living deep in the asteroid. And most likely, they were the killers.

We walked back quickly through the hallways of the station to the galley. I entered the galley to find Jones going through a cabinet of liquor while Vero sat at a table with her head in her hands. Ward leaned against the wall, watching the door.

"Hey Tommy," Jones said, waving a bottle in the air. "Spiced rum."

"You can't take it," Betti said.

"Why?" Jones said.

"It's compromised."

"Dammit, Betti. You really know how to ruin a man's night," Jones said, carefully placing the bottle back on the shelf. "Just when I thought something good might come out of this mission."

Vero stood up. "Are you ready to go back to the ship?"

"Yeah, but we can't quite yet," I said. "First, we need to set up some motion detectors."

"You want to see the leftovers?" Ward asked, a little too enthusiastically.

"Not particularly," I said. "Let's call into the ship and have Adler send our box of detectors out of the ship's airlock so we can grab them and set them up. Then we'll get out of here."

We got our stuff a half-hour later after directing Adler via the com. We installed the SensiTrac patch detectors at the entrance to the tunnel as well as in five other likely locations. We also popped some cameras into six additional locations, creating a small network that we could watch from the station. The cameras we had were tiny spy models, the size of a pin head. They came on a roll of tape. You peel off the backing, press a 2 centimeter square of tape to the wall, then peel it off leaving the little camera behind. It was a little tricky to do with the gloves on my battlesuit, but Ward found me a pair of needle-nose pliers that made the job easier.

After an hour our spy network was complete and we headed back to the ship. We were met inside the ship's airlock by the cleaning team. Dave and Ted. I could have shot them both for the pain-in-the-neck decontamination they put us through, though I knew it was necessary.

When the airlock opened, I was surprised to see what looked like a big plastic bag inside it.

"Who's first?" Dave asked over our com. "Ya'll are gonna have some fun!"

"Vero," I replied.

"Step into the bubble and we'll seal you in," Ted said, and she did. Then the airlock shut and we waited another ten minutes. Betti went next, then the doctor, then Zelag, Ward, Jones, and, after an hour of waiting, I stepped through into my own single-serving bag.

Once bagged, I had to lay on a cart and get wheeled down the hall into a small hermetic containment room with tiles on the floor. The rest of my team was already there, sitting on a bench, all still wrapped in plastic. It looked like the kind of place where you'd butcher pigs.

"Stand up," Dave said. I did, then they two of them rolled out the cart and sealed the door.

"So," Jones said. "We all gonna get naked?"

"Not yet," Dave said over the com. "But you can unzip your specimen bags. And keep your suits sealed."

"Great," Zelag said. "I'm a specimen now. I hate medical people."

I found the locks on the plastic and unzipped the seal. Jones simply ripped his off.

"I don't think you're supposed to do that," Betti said to him as she struggled with the zip on her seal.

"It's not like they're gonna reuse it," Jones said, reaching over and tearing the bag off her.

"True enough," came Dave's voice. "Now we're going to expose you to various forms of radiation, plus foam jets. You'll have to stand one at a time in the middle of the room."

"How long is this going to take?" Jones complained.

"Longer if you keep talking," Dave replied. "Who's first?"

Ward jumped up and stood in the middle of the room.

"Arms up," Dave said. "Legs apart."

Ward stood as told, then a deep hum came through the walls and there was a bright flash of white light, followed by a longer exposure of red light, then brilliant lasers played up and down over his suit—and after about a minute of that, jets emerged from the walls and soaked his suit in bubbling foam.

"It's like being in a skycar wash," Ward said as a rinse cycle started and washed the foam in rivulets from his pressure suit.

"Yeah," Jones said. "Too bad it's not a topless skycar wash." Betti thumped him in the arm with her fist and he laughed.

Finally, Ward was done.

"Walk on through the exit to the right for the next phase," Dave directed, and Ward walked out with a wave goodbye, then Vero stepped up.

I waited until everyone else was clear, then took my turn under the radiation and the cleansing foam. It didn't really feel like anything because the suit protected me from both the radiation and the disinfectant. Finally, the process was complete and I was permitted to walk through the doors. They sealed behind me and I was in a glowing red room, also covered in tile.

"Remove your suit and hang it in the corner," came Dave's voice. I did, stripping out of the suit and the specially designed waste-recycling undergarments inside it.

"Arms up, legs apart," Dave said over a speaker somewhere in the room. "And close your eyes and hold your breath. *Great, here we go again.* I assumed the stance and winced as a flash of light seared even through my eyelids, then I was suddenly awash in suds. The suds were followed by a warm and stinging liquid, then water, then finally jets of warm air which dried me off.

"Okay," Dave said. "Now you can walk through into the next room and grab a robe."

I walked into the next room and found a robe hanging on a hook. I put it on, then opened the door and found myself in one of the halls of the ship. Ted stuck his head out of a nearby doorway and grinned at me. "Feeling nice and fresh?" he asked.

"Sure," I said. "Like a new clone of myself."

"Great," he said. "We'll make sure your suits are all set for your next trip into the rock."

"Thanks," I said. "No hard feelings?"

"None at all," he said. He gave me a thumbs up and disappeared back into his room. By my calculations it had taken almost two hours for all of us to be decontaminated. I wondered if anything had been moving on the station. At least it was a lot quicker to travel onto the station than it was to come back. I could be suited up and out the airlock in about ten minutes if need be.

Whoever was left—provided they were still alive—would certainly be caught in our observation web. The decontamination procedures had taken my mind off the ship in part, but now everything was rushing back in a flood. We needed to nail those psychos and get out of here.

Chapter 13

I got dressed and picked up a cup of coffee from the galley, then met the rest of the team and set up an impromptu monitoring station in a cabin we'd requisitioned just two doors down from my own. Instead of feeling worn out, I was agitated and almost jumpy, like you feel when you drink too much caffeine on an empty stomach. I'd held myself together and didn't project any unease to my guys, but inside I was a mess of knots.

We stuck two big flatfoil screens up on a wall and Betti linked them up with our cameras. I'd set up twenty-four cameras and she had them going twelve to a screen. All of us had portable monitors that would sound an alarm if anything moved, but I couldn't stop watching. Over the course of a couple hours everyone else left but I sat almost in a trance, my eyes skipping from image to image. Alone in the cabin, I watched until my eyes blurred. I must have fallen asleep for a moment, because I woke with a jerk at one point, thinking I'd seen something... but there was nothing. Just the empty rooms and hallways of a dead station. It had been what... five hours, six hours since we'd been there? And still nothing. Maybe they *were* all dead.

I rubbed my eyes and got up. It wouldn't do any good to burn myself out. Smarter, not harder.

I went to my cabin with a little warning monitor in my pocket and set it on the desk next to my bed. I undressed, then lay on my back and stared at the ceiling, telling myself to calm down and sleep.

But sleep wouldn't come. Images flashed through my head of the long, dark tunnels cut into the asteroid. The strange words on the screen in the bridge. The thought of dismembered bodies in a freezer. A memory of Heiermach vomiting blood. The espionage agent with the bomb in his brain…

A soft knock at my door snapped me out of my dark reverie.

"Come in," I said. The door opened slowly, revealing Vero. She wore loose grey pajama bottoms and a black top. Her hair was a mess, like she'd been trying to sleep.

"I hope you don't mind company," she said.

"No, it's fine," I said, sitting up on the edge of my bed. She sat beside me in silence.

"Are you okay?" I asked after a moment.

"No," she said. "I'm in over my head."

"You're doing fine," I said.

She shook her head. "No, I haven't done well. I'm used to being in charge—to having everything together. This mission has me on pins and needles."

"Me too," I admitted. "It happens. We'll be out of here before you know it."

"I don't know how you're so calm," she said, leaning into my shoulder.

I put my arm around her and held her tight. We didn't say anything. I hadn't thought about her romantically—I mean, not more than noticing the size of her chest, the curve of her neck, her long legs, the smell of her hair and that sort of thing—but it was good to have some human contact after the insanity. If she needed a shoulder to lean on, I would lend it. And if she needed more, well…

She snuggled into my chest and I stroked her soft hair. The scent of her was starting to get to me. After a moment she looked up into my eyes. "You're tougher than I am, Tommy" she said, her eyes searching my face. "I'm scared. No, I'm terrified!"

I held her closer and she turned her face upwards as if leaning in for a kiss. I went to kiss her—and then her eyes turned red and she snarled at me. I frantically tried to push her away but her grip was like iron—and then I noticed her skin. Her face was starting to crack and blister! Like Heiermach!

"Vero!" I yelled and scrambled to escape her embrace. She snarled a gurgling snarl and curled her lips back, revealing a mouth filled with rows of teeth like the deadly maw of a shark. Saliva and blood dripped from her mouth.

Her hand snapped out and grabbed my throat, tearing into the skin of my neck. I lashed out and drove my palm up under her chin, knocking her off me. She hit the ground hard, but rolled back up to her feet. Under her pajamas her skin bubbled and oozed, fluids soaking through the thin fabric.

"Vero!" I yelled. "You're infected!"

She shrieked and jumped back on top of me but I kicked her off, throwing her into the wall, then leapt to my feet and looked for a weapon. Somehow, I had nothing—where was my rifle? Or even my Reaper?

She came back at me and I punched her full in the face, wincing as I felt her nose cave in. She fell to the floor on her back and I straddled her. She was spitting blood and shrieking—and still trying to tear at me with her claws. I pounded on her but she wouldn't stop. I hit her again and again until her features were a bloody pulp but she kept moving—and the horrible bubbling scream wouldn't stop—*dear god—just stop!!!*

Again and again and again I pounded my fists in her, the horror of what was happening twisting my guts. I pounded on her but she was still thrashing beneath me. The floor was covered in gore and every time I hit her she shrieked again, rhythmically, almost like the sound of an alarm, an insistent and never ending chime—over and over and over–

And suddenly I snapped awake. It was just a nightmare, a horrid, evil dream! But the sound, I wasn't imagining the sound! Then I realized it was coming from the alarm on the desk. The motion alarm! Someone was moving around the station!

I jumped out of my bunk and staggered into the monitoring room, still shaking with the aftereffects of the dream. Jones, Vero and Ward were already there. I gripped Vero's shoulder for a moment and she looked up at me. Her eyes were clear, her skin was smooth, and she was obviously fine. I shook my head and looked at the screens to see what was happening. Zelag and Betti stumbled in and joined us.

"Three of them!" Jones said, pointing to the image projected by camera 6. "They're in the cargo bay!"

"Jones, Ward and Zelag—suit up," I said, looking at three figured in vacc suits moving cautiously out of the cargo container obscuring the tunnel. "Let's get over there and nail these freaks!"

Chapter 14

"Make sure you don't kill them," Betti said over the com. "We need to know what's happened to those samples."

"No promises," Ward said. "If they try to eat me I'll blow their damn heads off."

"We'll do our best," I told Betti. "Keep an eye on them."

We entered the main airlock and moved cautiously down the main hall.

"Where are they, Betti?" I asked.

"They're heading for the galley," she replied. "They'll be there in just a moment."

"Probably looking for forks," Jones muttered darkly.

"We'll take them by surprise," I said. "Zelag, you and I will enter first, followed by Ward and Jones.

"Roger," Zelag said.

"They're in the galley now," Betti said. "They're removing their helmets and setting them on a cafeteria table."

I glanced at the station diagram on my visor. Almost there... we had them now.

We reached the door.

"They've gone through the cafeteria and are in the kitchen area," Betti said.

"Copy that," I said, then addressed the men. "We have them cornered in the kitchen. We can access it from the cafeteria. Let's go."

We walked into the cafeteria and found the lights had been turned on. I saw a couple of flashlights and three helmets on a table, just as

Betti had said. Zelag was at my shoulder with Jones and Ward behind. We reached the double doors of the kitchen and I held up a hand. Three. Two. One.

POW! I kicked the doors open and Zelag and I busted inside, rifles up. "Down on the ground!" I yelled, my battlesuit amplifying my voice. Two men and a woman were there—one of the men was in the middle of opening the fridge. All three spun around, jerkily, like there was something strangely wrong with them—and their faces looked off somehow. Then the guy at the fridge pulled out a laser cutter and fired a green beam that struck Zelag's shoulder. He shrieked in pain, causing Jones and Ward to burst charging into the room, and then we opened up on the bastards.

"STOP STOP STOP!!!" I heard Betti yelling over the com but it was too late. We riddled their torsos with lasers and plasma bolts, and all three hit the ground hard, as dead as their victims in the freezer. They'd shot first and we were jumpy as hell. No quarter!

"Alive!" Betti wailed. "We needed them alive!"

"Too late," I replied, collecting myself. My heart was in my throat. I looked at Zelag who was leaning back against the wall. "You okay?" I asked.

"I think I'll live," he said. His suit had already patched the hole with sealant. "Can't seem to move my arm properly," he said.

"Don't try," Ward said. "We'll get you back to the ship and take a better look. Hand tight."

"I have a lot of little baby guns at home that need me," Zelag said. "I'll try to hang on for their sake."

"Tommy," Jones said. "Those guys we shot are messed up."

"No way," I said sarcastically, turning around. "Close-range plasma fire will do that."

"No, it's not that," Ward said. "It's worse."

I moved closer at our victims and yeah, they were more than just a little weird. The skin of their faces was cracked and ulcerated. Two of them were gloveless and I saw the skin on their hands was also bad.

"What is it?" Zelag said from where he leaned against the wall.

"Nothing good," came Vero's voice over the com. "Betti says they're showing symptoms of a low dose of the *Exo-Ambystoma perhorridus* toxin."

"Salamander juice," Jones said.

"Made by a virus," Ward continued.

"Oh hell," Zelag muttered. "Do you think…"

He didn't finish the thought but we all knew what he was thinking.

"Avoid any additional exposure," Betti said over the com. "Doc wants to take samples—we're coming over."

"Roger," I replied. "Ward and I will come get you. Jones, stay here with Zelag."

Ward and I left the kitchen and walked silently down the hallway together. In a couple of minutes, we'd reached the airlock. We waited for Betti and Dr. Shutt for about ten minutes, then they arrived, carrying med bags.

"You shouldn't have killed them," the doctor said. "You have made our job harder."

"They shot at us," Ward replied.

Betti shook her head. "You were going to kill them anyway. You even joked about it."

"So what?" I said, defending Ward. "They shot first. This place is a house of horrors, complete with cannibals. It's all well and good to think about what you want to do when you're watching over the cameras but when you're in the middle of it, you're just trying to stay alive. And we did."

The doc shook his head and went into the kitchen.

"I'm sorry," Betti said. "I wasn't here. I'm sure you all did your best."

"Damn straight," I said.

We entered the galley and Betti joined the doc for a closer look at the bodies. Jones had Zelag sitting at a table now.

"You okay?" I asked the wounded man.

"Yeah, flying high. Whatever anti-pain drug they load into our suits has effectively neutralized the pain, though I have to say I would like a bit of that rum in the cabinet to take the edge off my nerves."

"Same here," I said. "I'll buy you something safer when we get back to Kantillon."

"Vero ID'd the bodies from my visor cam, Falkland," Jones said.

"Yeah?" I replied. "Who are they?"

"One was the station master. Everett Case. Another was a tech, I think. Jon Layton."

"The woman?" I asked.

"A scientist. Aila Thurston."

"Strange," I said. "I wonder what they were doing?"

"Probably a midnight snack," Zelag grunted.

"Geez," Jones said. "Don't remind me!"

The doctor emerged from the kitchen, closing up his bag, Betti behind him.

"Doc," I said. "Tell me—Zelag here—you think he'll get infected?"

"I'll let you know what I find," he said. "The victims have suffered exposure to the toxin at least, though certainly not a complete, intact strain of the virus." He patted his bag. "I'll know soon enough once I test these."

"Good," I replied. "You have everything you need, then?"

"Yes," he replied.

"Great," I said. "Let's get out of here."

"FALKLAND!" I jumped as Vero's voice shrieked over the com. "The alarm is going off again! Someone else just came out of the tunnel!!!"

Chapter 15

"Guys, you have to get him! And don't kill him this time!" Vero said. She was right, I knew. We needed answers. And this was just one guy. We could handle him.

"Jones, Ward, you two come with me," I ordered. "We'll ambush him in the hallway."

"We need to get Zelag back to the ship," Ward said.

"You're right," I said. "All right, you and Betti get him back to the ship, along with the doc. Jones and I will capture this last guy. Now get the hell out of here before he gets any closer!"

Ward went to help Zelag but he stood under his own power. "I'll be fine. I can run."

As they left I looked at the overview of the station inside my visor. I noted that Vero had already added the target's current location to the map. Good girl.

"Looks like I could get behind him by cutting through into the bridge along the crew dormitory hall, then cut back into the main passage from there," Jones said.

"Do it," I said. "I'll go straight down the hall and hang out in one of the side entrances just after the bend and let him approach." Jones took off. The target's location updated. Now he was in the hall before the bridge.

I ran down the hall about, then ducked into a small office off to one side before the hall took a curve. I could see Jones moving through the bridge and out into the hall. The target's last known location was maybe eight meters past the door to the bridge, still heading my way. I'd guessed he was heading towards the galley and I'd guessed right.

I stood still and listened, making myself breathe quietly and stay calm. Then I had a thought. Double-check we're non-lethal. I wouldn't make the same mistake we made on Feymanus. "Jones, make sure your rifle is on its lowest setting. And don't shoot me in the hallway or I'll kick your ass. I will engage first, and you nail him if he runs."

"Roger," he said. "I was already there."

Then I heard footsteps. Our target was closing. I counted to three and leapt in front of him, rifle at the ready. "Freeze!" I yelled and he stopped. He wore a vacc suit with the visor open. In one hand was what looked to be a cricket bat, in the other was a flashlight. He dropped the bat but held onto the light, a look of complete astonishment on his face.

"Wardogs?" he said. "Oh, thank God!"

That was the last thing I'd expected to hear. Most people were less than happy to see our distinctive red insignia.

"Take off your suit slowly and don't try anything," I said as Jones came up from behind. "We're going to search you for weapons."

"Absolutely, yes, oh, thank you," he replied, slowly unlatching his helmet.

"His skin looks okay," Jones said via our suit-to-suit com. I noticed the same thing. Unlike the people we'd shot earlier, this guy looked healthy. The stepped out of his suit and stood before us in a pair of boxers and an undershirt. "Pat him down," I said to Jones, and he did.

"He's clean," Jones said.

"All right," I said, then keyed my com to the ship. "Vero, we got him for you. Alive, this time. Sending you visor feed for ID."

"Good work," she said. "Okay, the system ID'd. That's Dr. Geirt Mortten. Researcher. Does he look sick at all? From here he looks fine."

"No," I replied. "Looks healthy."

"We need to interview him—please bring him to the ship. Dr. Shutt says the boys can keep him in a bubble."

"Roger," I said. "We'll be at the airlock in ten."

I turned towards our prisoner and set my voice for external. "Okay, Dr. Mortten, suit back up. You're coming with us."

"Thank you," he said. To my surprise there were tears in his eyes. "Oh, thank you so much! You saved my life!"

After another long and irritating decontamination—though I'm sure it was nothing compared to what they were putting the researcher through—I got a chance to grab some coffee and a reconstituted sub sandwich. I didn't realize how hungry I was until I started eating. Hunger really is the best seasoning.

Ward walked in, grabbed an energy drink and sat down next to me.

"Yo," he said. "Nice work not killing the guy. The girls say he's the last one."

"Thanks," I replied. "How's Zelag?"

"Fine so far," he said. "Deep burn into his shoulder. They'd taken the safety off the cutter. Caught him right at the joint, too. Lucky shot."

"I like the guy," I said.

"Yeah, he's solid," Ward said. That was high praise coming from him.

"You think he's gonna come down with whatever it is?" I asked.

"Dunno," he said. "Dr. Shutt says a blood test should tell him what's up. He's also very interested in the lab we found in the tunnel. He thinks they might have been refining the virus in there, maybe even farming the toxin for some reason by keeping the virus feeding on a medium. Chances are that's why the people we shot looked like hell," he said. "Improper handling in a makeshift lab."

"Geez," I said, tearing a strip off the top of my empty cup. "I wonder which came first—the crazy or the lack of safety? Like, did they accidentally mess themselves up a bit, then start eating people as they got battier—or were they so greedy to make their own side deal with the virus that they figured the risk was worth it, then got sucked into a cycle as they went psychotic, then maybe they–"

My thought was interrupted by the entrance of Jones. "Falkland— they're going to question the guy you brought in. Vero wants you in."

"Great," I said, standing and crumpling up my cup, then taking a shot at the recycler as I walked past. Missed.

"Zelag could've hit that," Jones said as I picked up the cup and chucked it in. "That is, unless he's a zombie by now."

"Don't even say it," Ward said. "Just don't."

"It was really late the night I first discovered everything was going straight to Hell," Mortten said from the other side of a translucent plastic bubble on one side of a small hospital room. His face was pale and there were dark circles under his eyes, but he still looked much better than the other people we'd seen before killing them. Vero, Betti, Jones and I occupied most of what remained of the room.

"I had a hunch that I could increase the viability of one of our strains by tweaking a particular glycoprotein in the viral envelope, so I was in the lab well past normal working hours running some simulations," he continued. "After multiple failures, I decided to call it a night. I shut down the lab and walked back to my cabin, turning over possibilities in my mind. I almost ran right into him! I hate to imagine what would have happened then."

"You almost ran into who?" Vero said.

"Everett," Mortten said.

"The station manager," Betti said.

"Right," Mortten said. "He had his back to me and was slipping into Andy's cabin."

"Andrew Carson, lead researcher," Betti interjected.

"How did you know it was Case?" Vero asked.

"He was wearing his uniform," Mortten said. "Black with yellow patches on the shoulders."

"And he went into Andy's room?" Vero said.

"Yes," Mortten replied. "He went in, then closed the door. He was moving slowly, sneaky like, and he had a cutter in his hand. I was a little ways off at the curve of the hallway, mind you, but that was suspicious as well. I mean, what's he going to do with a laser cutter in Carson's cabin in the wee hours of the morning? So I walked past my cabin and went right to the door. Then I heard the laser cutter engage, followed by a shriek of pain, then nothing. Scared the heck out of me!"

"So what did you do next?" Vero said.

"I ran like crazy, just hauled it down the corridor, grabbed a vacc suit, then through the cargo bay into the tunnels."

"Wait a minute," Jones said. "Why didn't you try to get help?"

"Are you kidding? The hallways are wide open and the cabins are locked at night. A psycho with a laser cutter and a skeleton key just murdered one of my friends in cold blood almost right in front of me! There was nothing I could do! I just ran and figured I'd come out again in the morning—the tunnels are a labyrinth and I knew I'd be safe."

"Yeah, about those tunnels," Vero said. "Why are they there? Who built them?"

"Beats me," Mortten said. "But they weren't exactly a secret."

"They weren't?" Jones asked.

"No, we all knew they were there. I think someone at corporate had an expansion in mind or something and it never got pulled off. Or actually, you know, they might have been there before they even bought the station. Poor Carson, you know, he told me once they'd bought the place from pirates some years back."

"Makes sense," Jones said.

"So you panicked and went into the tunnels," Vero said. "What did you do the next morning?"

"When my air started running low and I was beginning to wonder if I'd maybe dreamed the whole thing, I decided to head back into the station. I found some air in the cargo bay, then went down the corridor towards the cabins. That's when I realized things were seriously wrong."

"How so?" I asked.

"The lights were off, way past the normal sleep cycle. I could see with the vacc suit's light but I was freaked out. No one was in the hallways and the room doors were locked but I managed to get into Lisa's room, since I knew her code and we were... well, we were close."

He stopped for a moment and bowed his head. I saw a tear fall onto the front of his hospital gown, leaving a dark spot.

"And?" Vero prompted, gently.

"She was dead. On her bed. Her... there was a... a hole burned through her chest." He thumped his own chest. "Right here. He'd killed her too!" Mortten clutched his head in his hands. "Oh God..."

"It's not your fault," Vero said.

Morrten shook his head and made an obvious effort to pull himself together. "I can't excuse myself for being a coward. I was a coward!" he said.

"How so?" Vero asked.

"I could have run right to her cabin in the first place! I don't know when Case killed her. What if she was still asleep when I was running for the tunnels? What if I ran and left her to be slaughtered in her sleep?"

"You can't know that," Vero said. "You also could have been murdered yourself. Then no one would know what had happened or who had done it."

"Doesn't matter now," he mumbled. "It's too late. Oh, poor Lisa."

"So what did you do next?" Vero pressed.

"I left her cabin, feeling sick and more terrified than I've ever been in my entire life. I knew if I hung around the station, I'd be next. So I hauled it back to cargo bay, wolfed down some cold provisions I stole and refilled my oxygen, then turned to go back into the tunnel—and that's when I saw one of them."

"Who?" Jones asked.

"It was Layton. His face was broken out, skin cracking, you must know how they look now—he came in to the cargo bay, looked at me, and made this horrible face—like some sort of animal. And he was staggering and shaking. I ran into the tunnel, scared to death he'd catch me, locking my helmet on as fast as I could in the airlock—but he didn't follow. That time."

"What do you think happened to them?" I asked.

He shook his head. "Whatever happened, it turns normal people into psychopathic killing machines. Everett was a fine man. He was quiet, a bit of a stickler about regulations, but a normal guy. A good guy. Not the type of guy who would... well..." He paused and took a deep breath. "Anyhow, whatever they got, it does something to people's brains. I have some theories I can share later once I can get my own thoughts straight. For now, though, I'm just really glad you came when you did. I was going to wait until the next freighter arrived and hope to God they'd let me on board. I didn't expect to see anyone so soon—thank you so much, again, for coming in. I don't know who sent you but I feel like it must be the angels. My mother always told me angels were watching over us. I guess my angels must own stock in Wardogs."

"We're just here to help," Vero lied without hesitation. "Get some rest now, then we'll talk again soon."

"Any idea when I'll be out of here?" Mortten asked.

"As soon as all the tests are complete," Dr. Shutt said. "Probably by the end of the day."

"Thank you, doctor," he said fervently. "Thank you all—again."

We filed out of Mortten's room and headed to the ship's galley to decompress a bit.

"He's very upset about everything," Betti said, getting a cup of tea. "Highly stressed."

"Yeah," Vero said. "Obviously. He spent a lot more time in there than we did and I'm a mess." She hunted around the kitchen. "Dammit! I would kill for a vodka and cranberry juice right now."

I got a coffee with extra cream and sugar to cover the lousy flavor. Ward walked in and grabbed an energy drink.

"Learn anything interesting?" he asked.

"We'll fill you in later," Vero replied. "It's time to get the hell out of here. Tommy, you, Jones and Ward are up for the final cleanup?"

"What kind of cleanup?" I asked.

"THI now wants us to transfer all the bodies and put them in cold storage before we blow the place. Betti and Elsie have already downloaded the station's computer network, so once we have the remains locked down, we can blow the place to hell and collect our pay."

"Wait," Ward said. "I thought THI just wanted us to kill everyone and shut things down?"

"Look, I am not asking questions, here!" Vero snapped. "This is what they want and I don't want to hang around this place one second longer than I have to! Get the bodies, blow the place, turn everything over to THI, and we never come back again!"

"Fine," Ward said. "It's about damn time to blow it up. I just don't see why the—"

"Ward, not now," I said. I could see Vero was going to lose it and I wanted to get out of here almost as badly as she did. "Jones, Ward, let's eat, then we can suit up and play undertakers."

"No problem," Jones said. "If they weren't paying us, I'd pay THI for the chance to blow the place up."

"Same here," I said. "You game, Ward?"

"Hell yes," Ward replied. "Dibs on the detonator."

Chapter 16

We put each corpse into its own specimen bag and borrowed the forklift from the cargo bay to carry them through the hallways to the airlock. It was a nasty job and the corpses had deteriorated significantly—yet our desire to get out was all-consuming. Each specimen bag and its gruesome contents was moved into the airlock, then double-bagged in vacuum, then taken through the decontamination room, then moved into the medship's spacious morgue freezer.

After a few hours we'd moved them all, then we set charges. Lots of charges. Jones was actually whistling as he worked.

Finally, we were done. Then we had to go through the entire obnoxious decontamination routine again.

Ward hit the button as we watched from the ship's bridge 30,000 kilometers away. All of us were there, including Zelag. To his great relief, he'd been declared infection-free and his shoulder was going to heal. He stood against the back wall, his arm in a sling, a grim smile on his face as he watched the screen. Blowing this place up felt like Christmas. When Ward punched it, the zoomed view on the screen was the most beautiful thing I'd seen in a long time. Blasts of light and steam shot from various points of the asteroid base, rolling across the rock. The pattern of destruction spread like a wave and climaxed as the whole rotten place exploded into a million molten pieces.

Asteroid 30193 G-S was no more.

Jones pumped his fist. *Goodbye and good riddance*, I thought.

I caught Vero looking at me and I looked back, holding her gaze. She smiled slightly and smoothed her hair as she looked away. This mission had shaken her to the core and she was now relying on me to keep herself together. I thought about that look and wondered if there might be a chance to get a little closer on the return voyage.

Dr. Mortten had been cleared to leave his bubble and stood with us on the bridge. He watched the expanding chunks of asteroid with no expression on his face. The dude probably had nothing left to feel— he'd been through the wringer and it might take a long time for him to get his life back. He was lucky to be alive at all, I thought. Especially considering our first goal was to simply kill everyone. Even though he'd lived, he'd still been involved in making some nasty shit. Maybe this would wake him up.

"Well," Jones said. "Who's up for champagne?"

"I don't like the way he looks at me," Vero said as we all sat together in the galley. Our team was nursing some drinks in disposable cups. We hadn't found any cranberry juice but Zelag had "found" a few bottles of gin somewhere. On ice it was drinkable, though it was far from my first choice.

"Who, me?" Jones said. He's been paying attention to a highlight reel from a zero-grav baseball game playing on the screen above the counter.

"No," Vero said. "Well, yes, but not like Mortten."

"He's a mess," Ward said.

Betti nodded. "I don't like him either."

"Women never like the sciency types," Jones said. "And he cried like a pussy over his poor, lost Lisa."

"I wouldn't be too hard on him," Ward said. "He's been running from psychotic cannibals with plague or something. Probably glad to have something nicer to look at for a change."

"Yeah," I agreed, giving Vero a sidelong glance. "Much nicer."

She grinned at me, the first real smile I'd seen on her face in a while. "Nicer than burned bodies and cracking skin?" she said. "You really know how to charm a girl."

I shrugged, not taking the bait.

"Whelp," Jones said, slugging his drink. "Anyone want to kill some zombies?"

"You got it set up?" Ward said.

"Yep," he replied. "Rec room screen. Four players, if we have any takers. Betti—you want to join us?"

Betti smiled at him. "Thought you'd never ask."

"You, Falkland?" Jones said.

"Naw," I said. "I think I've killed enough zombies on this trip."

"I'd play but I'm a little short-handed," Zelag shrugged, then winced. "Yeah, definitely short-handed. I'm going to hit the sack."

"Suit yourself," Jones said, taking Betti's hand and walking out with her and Ward. Zelag waved good night with his cybernetic hand, leaving me alone with Vero.

Vero poured herself another shot of gin and shook her head. "I never liked this stuff all that much. Dad used to drink it, but I thought it tasted like aromatic hydrocarbons." She took a swig. "It's good now, though."

"This mission could make isopropyl palatable," I said.

"Yeah, but you held it together," Vero said, taking my hand. "I keep having nightmares and feeling like I'm on the edge of disaster. Betti woke me up in the middle of the night last night because I was moaning in my sleep. You're handling everything fine, though—even back on Feymanus. I feel like you give me strength. You kept me sane."

"All in a day's work," I said. "Though I'm not exactly sleeping well myself."

She squeezed my hand. "You know, this may not be very professional of me, but maybe..."

"Maybe what?" I said. I knew where this was going and I liked it.

"Oh, I don't know," she said.

"Veronique," I said, looking into her eyes. "I'm getting tired, so let's make a deal."

"A deal?" she said.

"Yes," I replied. "I'd like to make sure we both get a good night's sleep."

"Oh really?" she said.

"Yes," I replied. "Really."

"And how would you make that happen?"

"Well," I said. "I'm going to let you stay in my room tonight, but you have to promise me something."

"What?" she said.

"Pinky promise you won't take advantage of me."

"What?" she said, batting her eyes. "Moi?"

I held her hand tighter. "See, there's only one bed. I'm just afraid you might want a backrub to relax your nerves. Then, you know how things go."

"Sounds like you're going to take advantage of me," she said.

"Never," I said.

We were barely inside my cabin and Vero was already running her hands under my shirt and kissing me. I ran my own hands up inside her blouse as I hugged her close, running my fingers over the soft curve of her back. She kissed me harder and pulled me tight, then I pulled her shirt over her head—and a horrible thought popped into my head which completely threw me out of the moment. "The bodies in the freezer," I blurted.

Her jaw dropped open and she pushed me away. "What, Tommy? Why the hell would you bring that up!?"

"They were butchered," I continued. *Dammit, Tommy.*

"Properly."

"WHAT?" Vero said, a look of mingled shock and disgust on her face. "I cannot believe you just said that!" She stood there in just her slacks and bra, looking hot as thermite.

But I had to finish my thought. "They were cut up neatly, not like something those whacked-out, poisoned survivors would have done.

Plus, if those three survivors were eating the bodies, they weren't eating enough."

"Wait, what do you mean?" Vero said, her expression softening into a more pensive one. "Are you saying–

"I'm saying we are not dealing with people crazed by an infection."

"Of course we were," Vero said. "They were chasing down Mortten, the station master's log was full of weird stuff and he was killing people in their sleep. What else would make sense?"

You know when you don't want to say something, because you feel like saying it is going to make it happen? That's what I felt like just then. You know, like the old vet that doesn't want to say "this could be it" when he's heading out on one last mission, just because the very act of saying it might make it the end. That's what I felt like. But I had a bad feeling that was gnawing at me and trusting my bad feelings has kept me alive more than once or twice. Vero looked up at me and I had to spit it out or choke. So I spit it.

"Vero, what if we killed the wrong people?"

"Of course you killed the wrong people," Vero said. "I mean, you killed the right people, but at the wrong time."

"No," I said. "I mean, what if the three survivors who took a shot at Zelag were hunting down the uninfected survivor?"

"You mean they were hunting Mortten?" Vero said.

"Right," I replied. "What if he is the killer and they had survived him somehow? Maybe they were the last people who could have told us what really happened."

"Oh, Hell no," Vero said, putting her hand to her mouth. "If you're right, then we have a cannibal psycho wandering around the *St. Roch* right now! But there's no way to know anymore, is there? The others are all dead!"

"Yeah," I said. "We lost our best chance to find out when we got too trigger-happy."

"Wait," Vero said. "Maybe they can still tell us."

"How?" I said.

"The man and the woman that were butchered," she said, grabbing her shirt and throwing it on. "There should be DNA evidence on them. We need to get to the freezer and take samples. We've still got the killer's leftovers."

"You know, cutting up frozen corpses has never been on my top ten list of great dates."

"Me either," she said. "But there's no way in hell I'm waiting around to get drilled through the chest in the middle of the night."

"Or eaten," I added, buckling on my holster and Reaper. "Should we wake the others?"

"No," Vero decided. "Not yet. Let's run the test without telling anyone else. We don't actually know anything yet, not at this point."

"Agreed," I said.

We walked past the cabin Vero shared with Betti, then saw the "do not disturb" light on the door. I heard a girlish giggle from inside. Good job, Jonesie. Apparently killing zombies had taken a romantic turn.

"I was thinking of getting my Bobcat," Vero said. "But never mind. You can cover us both. Besides, you never know when I might accidentally pull the trigger six times in a row."

"We'll be fine," I said. "Concentrate on the medical stuff."

The morgue was next to the lab, so we headed there and found the drawer where the leftover human steak had been stored. There was the half-finished meal, still in its plastic container. *Waste not, want not*, I thought, with a shiver.

Vero grabbed the leftovers and we headed to the lab. We suited up in scrubs and gloves from the lockers, then Vero powered up the scanner and hooked in to the lab's AI. I watched as she carefully removed one of the half-chewed pieces of rare meat and sliced off a tiny sample with a scalpel, then put it onto a tray and slipped it into the scanner.

The screen above started displaying information and I watched without understanding as readouts appeared. This was outside my expertise but Vero was in her element.

"Here it comes," she said. "We're getting two distinct sets of DNA now. In a minute we should have a positive ID."

I leaned in to look.

"What are you working on?" a voice said from behind us. I wheeled to face the intruder.

It was Mortten!

Chapter 17

"We're just running a test," I said, reaching for my Reaper.

"It was you!" Vero gasped, looking at the image that had just appeared on the sequencer's screen. Mortten's face!

I yanked my gun out but Morrten had leapt towards Vero and I didn't dare fire. He snarled and tackled her to the ground, grabbing her by the neck, his mouth open. He was trying to bite her face! I lashed out with my boot and kicked him in the ribs, sending him sprawling, but he came up again with a knife and slashed at me. I stepped sideways, caught his wrist and jerked his arm forward with my right hand as I smashed my left forearm against his locked elbow. There was a loud crack as the bone snapped. He shrieked in pain and released the knife, thrashing around as I tried to take him down and incapacitate him.

"Help!" I heard Vero shriek over the lab com. "We're in the lab—Mortten has gone full psychotic!"

The psycho bit my left arm as I tried to lock him up and I cursed him as I pulled my other fist back and smashed him hard in the face. That knocked his teeth out of arm and laid him out on his back. Stunned, he made as if to get up again, but I grabbed him by the face and repeatedly slammed his head down on the metal decking until he quit moving, out cold, with my blood on his mouth. I stood over him, blood dripping blood from my arm, which is how Zelag and Ward found me when they rushed into the lab, their weapons at the ready.

"He went after you!?" Ward said, looking at the nicely tenderized form of Mortten on the floor. "After we saved his ass?"

I nodded and Zelag saw my arm, then looked down at the unconscious lunatic. "What the hell? Did he bite you?"

"He went after me first," Vero sobbed. "Tommy kicked him off me."

Jones came in, shirtless, followed by Betti in something transparent. "What's going on?" Jones said, his 3011 in his hand.

"Mortten attacked us," I explained. "Look at the screen there. He's the cannibal!"

Joens glanced at the man's profile picture on the screen, an older official ID image of Morrten with a half-grin.

"We got his DNA from some of the flesh he left in the fridge," Vero said. "We were testing it when he jumped us."

"I told you he was always looking at us strangely!" Betti elbowed Jones.

Jones pointed his blaster at Mortten's chest. He was breathing shallowly but he was definitely still out. "Bye-bye, psycho," he said.

"Wait," Vero said. "You can't do that!"

"Wanna bet?" I said.

"Give us one good reason, Parey," Ward demanded.

"Takamoto," she said.

"What?" I said. "So what about them? You think they'd thank us for saving a cannibal psycho? Weren't we supposed to neutralize everyone on the station?"

"Yes," she said, still trying to catch her breath. "But you're missing the point. Remember what they did to Hozumi?"

"Their investigator?" Zelag said.

"Oh, right," I said, suddenly realizing what Vero was getting at. "They killed him to tie up their loose ends. And they were going to have us wipe the station clean to get rid of more of those loose ends."

"Exactly," Vero said. "And killing him would leave us as the only loose ends left. We know who was refining the toxin and was going to sell it—the station manager and the other survivors. The viruses they were working with hadn't made it off the station yet, since the fake accident in the lab happened after the most recent ship appeared. That's when the samples disappeared. This guy is the last loose end left and we're going to turn him over to Takamoto—let them get the whole story out of him. We're just the muscle, right? Who's to say we figured out what's going on. No, if we kill him, they don't get their scapegoat."

"But if we turn him over to them, we give them a nice cover story," Betti added. "You make a lot of sense."

"Damn," Jones said. "You make a lot of sense. What do you think, Tommy?"

"They're right," I said. "He's our insurance policy."

Jones and Zelag both nodded. But Ward shook his head.

"I'm not keen on letting him wake up on the flight home," he said. "Who knows what trouble he could cause. Think we could stick him in stasis?"

"He bit Tommy," Jones said. "That means Tommy's gonna turn zombie next. We should probably ice him too."

"Shove off," I said.

Captain Teller came in, followed by Dr. Shutt and one of the crew medics.

"Just the folks we needed to see," Vero said. "This man attacked us, but he's been dealt with and needs to be delivered alive to THI. Can one of you plug him into a medical stasis unit—a gelpack, maybe—until he can be turned over to our client?"

"Sure," said the medic. "What the hell did you do to him?" he asked, then saw my arm. "Whoa, you need to get that cleaned up. That's a bite!"

"Yeah," I said. "Just deal with him first. He's probably concussed. I knocked his head on the floor a few times. Keep him alive but don't let him wake up."

The crewman nodded, then called for backup on his suit com, then turned to me again. "Put some pressure on that arm. You need to get to the clinic."

"No problem," I said. "I'll be there in a few." Vero got me some disinfectant and a wad of gauze from a supply closet, then I sat on the countertop and watched a few med guys put a neck brace on Mortten and take him out on a stretcher.

"What made you think to come down to the lab tonight and run the DNA?" Ward asked once the crewmen were gone.

"I don't know," I said. "A gut feeling."

"Lucky guess," Jones said.

"Yeah. It was. But I wasn't as lucky tonight as I thought I'd be," I said under my breath, nodding my head towards Vero as she sat at the sequencer with Dr. Shutt.

"No other DNA on any of these samples," Vero said, not seeing me look at her. "All Mortten."

"And he wasn't even the one working in the rigged up lab," Shutt added. "No sign of the toxin in him."

"Just a straight-up psycho," Vero said. "Scary, though."

"Yeah," I agreed. "Scary."

Chapter 18

After we turned Morrten over to Takamoto's Director of Security on Mordas Prime, we caught a regular liner back to Kantillon since WDI didn't have any ships available in the system. THI paid WDI and we each got a nice chunk sent to our bank accounts. Once we were in-system we called in to HQ. Captain Marks picked up the call himself and told us to head straight to Kookooma as a team and use the rest of our vacation. "Decompress," he said. "Spend some of that hard-earned cash. I'll be in touch soon. For now, play some games, chase some girls, and grill some steaks on the beach." When he said that, I thought of the prime cuts we'd found in the space station's fridge and decided to stick with the seafood.

Betti and Vero came along, but they went their own way when we hit the surface. I was looking to see if Vero and I could pick up where we left off that crazy night on the *St. Roch*.

"We were this close," I told Jones, holding my thumb and forefinger a centimeter apart. Ward and Zelag were off playing games while Jones and I sat at a little cafe table overlooking the beach. It was mid-evening and the breeze was warm and the sound of the waves relaxing. Soft music played from the tiki bar behind us as slowly changing colored lights lit up the coconut palms. I took a deep swig of my beer and watched a pair of girls in bikinis walk past in the dappled light.

"Too bad you had to start thinking about corpses in freezers," Jones laughed, draining his Newt and holding up two fingers at a server. "And you think I'm bad with women. Ha!"

"I never said that," I said.

"Betti was a great lay," he said. "It was practically a threesome, thanks to Elsie. I had her read out loud from Gorta's *Betelgeusian Sutra* while Betti and I did it."

"Liar," I said.

The server brought us another round.

"Honest truth," he said. "Would a pope lie to you? And man, she was really a goer, too. And a yeller."

"Just rub it in," I said. "Dammit. You know, I already had Vero's shirt off before we raced off to the lab. She's exactly my type, too. We were really getting along, and I don't just mean that night."

"Vero's a little old for you, though, isn't she?"

"No, not that old," I protested. "She's only in her 30s, I think. And she's fit. And hot."

"Yeah," Jones said. "I wouldn't mind a slice of that myself."

"You stay away from her," I said. "We're going to settle down and have 3.3 children and a nice conservative family skycar. I'm going to pick out some dishes and get a picket fence and everything. She's mine, Jonesie."

"Who's yours, Falkland?" came a familiar voice. Vero! I turned to see her and Betti standing at our table, in full corporate uniforms. I'd barely seen them since we arrived.

"No one," I said. "Nothing."

"What are a couple of nice ladies like you doing in a place like this?" Jones said, winking at Betti. I noticed she didn't wink back.

"We've been ordered to Rhysalan," Vero said. "Legal emergency. Apparently a Wardog ran into a jurisdiction issue with His Grace's Military Crimes Investigative Division and we've got to go clear it up."

"Great," I said. "And you need a bodyguard?"

"No," Vero said. "But thanks for the offer. Don't get in trouble, now."

"Wait," I protested. "You're just going to leave, just like that?"

She shrugged. "Duty calls. It's been fun, boys. We'll see you around sometime."

Betti blew us a kiss and the two of them walked off together.

"Cold," Jones said.

"Cold as space," I said. "Damn."

"Easy come, easy go," Jones said.   "Hey, think there are any Achernaran girls here tonight?"

"I think I've had enough dangerous blue things," I said.

"I dunno," Jones said. "Toxic salamanders are a far cry from nice, warm women. I wonder if their tongues are blue as well. Do you think they can suntan? Or if their butts are blue? I'm going to ask the next one I see."

"They're blue all over, Jones. And I'll bet they get tired of being asked questions like that, you know."

"You're just bitter because you're no good with girls," Jones said.

"Hey now," I said. "Just because you got with Betti and I blew my shot doesn't mean you're the man. In fact, you're nothing but a–"

Then Jone's com and mine beeped at the same time.

"New message," I said, keying the message up on my retina. "Captain Marks."

"Yep," Jones said. "Same here. Another gig. Hmm. A cakewalk, he says."

"Yeah, right," I groaned.

"Hey," Jones said. "Couldn't be any worse than these last two, right? First nukes, then cannibals. What's next, Unity AIs?"

"You just *had* to say it, didn't you," I said, putting my head in my hands.